THE

TRUTH

IS

DEAD

**WALKER
BOOKS**

THE TRUTH IS DEAD

This collection first published 2010 by Walker Books Ltd
87 Vauxhall Walk, London, SE11 5HJ

2 4 6 8 10 9 7 5 3 1

This book has been typeset in Fairfield LH

Printed and bounded in Great Britain by Clays Ltd, St Ives plc

British Library Cataloguing in Publication Data:
a catalogue record for this book is available from the British Library

ISBN 978-1-4063-2003-9

www.walker.co.uk

CONTENTS

Introduction, *by Marcus Sedgwick*   7

Jesus Wept, *by Anthony McGowan*   13

The Burning Glass, *by Marcus Sedgwick*   27

Vienna, 1912, *by Mal Peet*   55

The Blue-Eyed Boy, *by Linda Newbery*   69

Eclipsed, *by Matt Whyman*   83

One Giant Leap, *by Philip Ardagh*   95

The Y2K Bug, *by Eleanor Updale*   109

At the Ball Game, *by Frank Cottrell Boyce*   129

INTRODUCTION

The truth is dead. Or, at least, after these short attacks upon it, lies seriously, perhaps fatally, wounded.

What follows are eight examples of stories sometimes described as "counterfactual" – that is, they take an event in history and consider how things might have turned out if one or two factors has been just that little bit different. There is a long and noble tradition of playing around with the facts in this way: the "winners" in history – the guys with the biggest swords, the nastiest guns and often the worst sense of humour – have, after all, always indulged their imaginations to a degree. The history they tell is sometimes true, but only from a certain point of view.

Collecting these tales has been a wonderful and enjoyable process, and as an author I can give them no higher compliment than to say that I wish I'd written every one of them myself. Including my own – which was actually written by the team of eager monkeys I keep locked in my cellar. ("No story? No banana!")

The great thing about this type of story is that it's simply a lot of fun wondering, What if...? Now, obviously, this is only interesting if you know which episode in history has been tampered with. Some of the stories in this anthology relate to very well-known moments, others to those less well known. There are explanations along the way to fill in some gaps – but if you need telling that the moon didn't explode in the 1980s, then maybe this isn't the book for you...

The stories appear in chronological order and span a couple of thousand years of human history. We start a good long time ago, in the desert with that most famous of carpenters: Jesus. Anthony McGowan's story focuses on the period in Jesus's life when he wandered through the desert for forty days and forty nights and was tested and tempted by the Devil.

Our next story – my own – takes us to nineteenth-century Europe. It centres on Napoleon, the short and apparently rather stroppy French emperor who ruled most of the Continent for a decade or so, having made his name as a military commander in the years before and during the French Revolution. After a series of defeats, Napoleon was forced to abdicate and was sent to live in exile on the island of Elba. But, as you will see when you read my story, he never stopped scheming about ways to make his comeback…

I can't go into too much detail about our next two stories without giving the game away, but I will say that their choice of subject is very interesting and significant for subsequent history. The first of these, Mal Peet's story, is set in pre-World War One Vienna. The Austrian capital was at that time an extraordinarily fertile place, both culturally and otherwise, full of people who were to have a major impact on the twentieth century. Mal has chosen to write about perhaps the most famous one of all...

The second, Linda Newbery's tale, takes us onto the battlefields of France in 1914, at the beginning of the First World War. It is difficult to comprehend the number of men killed in the four-year conflict – an estimated eight million died and millions more were injured. Linda gives an insight into that bloody war and tells how the fate of one soldier was to change the course of history.

Next up is Philip Ardagh. His tale brings us ever closer to the real fascination of the counterfactual story as we discover how the history we take for granted could so easily have turned in a different direction. Taking inspiration from a genuine historical document – one that was written but, in the course of events, never used – Philip has chosen to retell the events of the 1969 moon landing.

The moon is also the subject of Matt Whyman's story – although it has a very different role to play here, as you will see. An embittered stand-off between the United States of America and the Communist Soviet Union over the development of nuclear weapons, part of what was known as the cold war, had dominated global politics since 1945. By the 1980s there was a very real fear that the conflict would escalate into a nuclear Armageddon. If war did break out, the British would have only a four-minute warning – the estimated time it would take for a Russian missile to reach the UK – before the world ended.

As the close of the twentieth century approached, global paranoia turned in a different direction: what would happen to the world's computers when the clock struck midnight on 31 December 1999? Eleanor Updale draws on those fears in her contribution. Stories like this show just how easily the foundations of our society could slip away.

And for our final tale what could be more appropriate than a good bleak end-of-the world conspiracy theory? (And, heaven help any future historians if this mischievous book is the only record of the last two thousand years to survive that end!) Frank Cottrell Boyce's story exploits this idea with his tale about the Aztecs. Suppose the Europeans had not decimated the Aztec civilization back in the sixteenth century, but rather that those Aztecs had conquered Europe. And suppose still further that their first conquest had been the village of Glasgow…

The only other thing you need to know is that according to some interpretations of Aztec mythology, the world is due to end in 2012. (On 21 December, to be precise, in case you want to set a reminder on your phone.)

I hope you enjoy reading these stories as much as I enjoyed collecting them.

Marcus Sedgwick

JESUS WEPT

Anthony McGowan

According to the Gospels of Matthew, Mark and Luke in the New Testament, Jesus wandered in the desert for forty days and forty nights, during which time he was tempted by the Devil…

That sandal was really bugging Jesus. Part of him knew it was insane to get annoyed by a mere sandal, given the fact he was alone in the wilderness, with nothing to eat but locusts – not the juicy ones, mind, but dry desert locusts; he'd have got more goodness out of that blasted sandal – and nothing to drink but dew, lapped up off the bare rock where it formed in the morning.

And then there was that whole heavy thing about what he was supposed to be doing with the rest of his life. Going up to people and telling them to throw down their nets or whatever and leave their families and follow him, because he – and this was the part that really made him cringe – *HE WAS THE SON OF GOD*. What sort of job was that?

And beyond that, he knew there was something much, much worse. A time of necessary pain and death. He could have looked into the future more carefully and truly *seen* what was coming, but he denied himself that knowledge. It was cheating.

So perhaps that's why he was obsessing over the sandal. Because all the other things he could think about were *way* more depressing than a broken strap and a sole that flapped like a loose sail in a storm on the Sea of Galilee.

Jesus poked at the strap. There was probably a special tool for fixing those things. A sandal spangler, or strap thribber, something like that. His father would have known. His father would have fixed the cursed object in five seconds flat. He'd have held it up to his eye, turned it round, figured out exactly what had to be done, and got those strong brown fingers of his working. Joseph had been good with stuff. Jesus the klutz, on the other hand, was always whacking his thumb with the hammer, or accidentally nailing his hand to a plank in the workshop.

A tear spilled from his eye, rolled down his nose and plopped into the sand at his feet as he thought about the old man, dying, worn out before his time.

And then a faint yet oddly penetrating voice reached Jesus through his thoughts.

"You, hey, wait."

It was the first human voice he'd heard in all the forty days and forty nights of his desert fast.

He turned and gazed back down the rock-strewn slope. Squinting into the sun he saw a figure scrambling towards him. Sweat stung his eyes, and Jesus drew the dirty sleeve of his garment across his face. He thought about his mother, who had made the robe from a single piece of soft cloth, its seams so cunningly wrought as to be almost invisible.

"Hotter than hell here."

The voice again. The man still toiled towards him. Even at this distance there was something bizarre about his appearance. His clothes were strange, following his contours in obscene dark unflowing detail. A Roman fashion? Or something from the East? Jesus blinked, and somehow – no doubt a trick played by fatigue, hunger, the relentless sun – the figure was there before him.

And what had appeared strange at a distance, now became bizarre, and frightening. And it wasn't just the dark suit, or even the shining black patent leather shoes, or the unnatural white of the shirt, or the shimmering iridescent blue of the tie. For the man had no eyes. Or rather, where his eyes should have been were two mirrors fastened with a metal frame to the man's face.

And in those mirrors Jesus saw himself. Saw the bones in his face where the flesh had shrunk, saw his own eyes deep in his skull, saw the hair filthy and matted. Saw, or thought he saw, a circle of thorns around his head and lines of blood like red tears.

"For a guy with a broken sandal, that's some pace you set there. And while we're on the subject, why don't you let me get that for you?"

And on the feet of Jesus there were no longer the tattered

worn sandals, but a soft enclosing mesh of some unknown white material, and an undulating sole that held his foot as gently as a cloud.

Jesus closed his eyes, knowing that in his delirium the time of temptation had come. He kicked off the outlandish shoes and sent them skittering away down the slope, where they turned to stones.

"Nike no good? You want Puma? Adidas?"

Jesus ignored him. In bare feet now, he continued to walk up the mountain, relieved, almost, that it had begun.

"OK, so you got me," said the man, his short legs scuttling to keep up with the steady tread of Jesus. "No one ever said you weren't smart. Look, it's too hot for all this tearing about on mountains. It ain't like we're a couple of kids. Let's sit down and talk about it in a civilized way. You know I've got to do this, so we may as well get it over with as soon and as painlessly as possible. Just give me ten minutes to hit you with my spiel, then you can tell me to get stuffed and we can get on with the rest of our ... well, with the other things we have to do. You're a busy guy; I'm a busy guy. Busy busy busy. The stuff I've got on, you wouldn't believe. War, crime, murder – one damn thing after another."

And Jesus felt suddenly the great sadness of everything, like the weight of death on his shoulders, and he wanted more than anything to sit and rest.

"Look, here's good," said the man, showing with his hand a flat rock. He pulled a red spotted handkerchief from his sleeve and dusted the rock. Then he sat and patted the space beside him, and Jesus sat also.

"Heck of a view," the man said. "You can see clear to…" He waved vaguely, and Jesus saw his nails, perfect and clean and sharp. "Well, over there."

The sun was lower in the sky and the desert was burning red. Shadows like long knives crawled over the land.

Then Jesus noticed that the bare rock on which he had sat was now black leather. He sank deeply into the softness. He tried to struggle up, but his weariness was too great, and the delicious enveloping comfort too welcoming. He thought that no one, not even Herod in his palace or Caesar in Rome, had ever known a seat like this.

"That's more like it," the man said. "OK, look, like with any deal, any contract, there's two sides to this. There's what I have to offer, and what I want in return. I'm guessing there's no point in me dangling all the usual stuff before you: the riches, the power, the kingdoms? But they're on the table if you want them. I'm not saying you should take them for the kicks you'll get, but, well, you know a guy like you with real power could do a lot of good. I mean, who would you rather have in charge of an empire, you or Caligula? Or, thinking ahead a little, my boys Genghis, Tamburlaine and Adolf? Irresponsible not to have a go, when you think about it. Like they say, all that's necessary for the triumph of evil is that good men do nothing, and you're just sitting there kinda doing nothing, bud. Well…?

"No, fine, didn't think you'd bite on that one. Temporal power not your thing. I get it. Render unto Caesar that which is Caesar's, blah blah blah. So, maybe a bit of the *other*. Man, you should see the babes I could fix you up with. Built like goddesses. Hey, some of them *are* goddesses! And I don't just mean the chicks around now; I'm talking about every beauty that has ever lived or will ever live.

"No? Not girls. *Boys*, maybe? OK, keep your hair on. Don't get your knickers in a twist; I was just asking. Live and let live, I say. Still *nyet*? Well, that's what I reckoned. But you know how it is. I had to ask. If I didn't follow the script, there'd be hell to pay."

Through all this Jesus had remained impassive. Resisting temptation was his job, just as the role of the Father of Lies was to tempt.

"But that's not all I've got here," the man continued. "And we're going multimedia with this one."

He drew a rectangle with his finger in the air, and where he drew, a dark shape appeared, like a window into emptiness.

"I want you to watch this. Because the thing is, I know you're a good guy. Hey, one of the best. No, *the* best. Your heart's in the right place. No arguments there. You want things to work out well. You want the little people to be OK. I've read the book. Love thy neighbour, turn the other cheek, blessed are the cheesemakers, all that stuff. Who's gonna argue with that? If you were thinking of starting up a religion, then that's exactly the sort of material you'd want in there. But, well, the best-laid plans of mice and men, and... No, look, let's just watch the movie. A picture's worth a thousand words. Let me wind this on to the right place … yeah, here we go."

Images appeared on the floating screen. There was music. There were voices. To Jesus it was all meaningless. Except that he could make out scenes of horror. Blood. The only meaning was blood. He closed his eyes.

"Oh, crap, I should have known you'd be a bit freaked by the technology. So why don't I just talk you through what's happening here? You know, like the extras on a DVD, when the director gives you his commentary. Except you don't know. Anyway, with what I'm saying, and what you can see, you'll get it. Get it? Cool."

Jesus opened his eyes. The sun was below the horizon and the yellows and reds of the desert were turning grey and blue. It was a beautiful time. Cooler now than the terrible heat of the day, but warmer than the wretched cold of the desert night. He had tried to light fires, but that was not his skill, and so he had shivered and moaned like a fanatic through the cold black hours.

"Right, here we go. Your people, the people you pick, good men mostly. Except Ju— Well, let's not get ahead of ourselves. But things start going pear-shaped pretty soon after you quit the scene. First your guys go and upset the Romans – and believe me, that's never a good idea. Hang on, let me…"

He fished down the side of the leather sofa until he hit on the remote control, but not before he'd also found – and discarded in frustration – a number of coins, a box of matches, a hairbrush and a fluff-covered object that might once have been a gummy bear.

"Right, let's fast-forward until … here you go."

The screen showed a Roman amphitheatre. A family – a mother and a father, a boy and a girl – kneeling in the sand. A lioness, hungry, wary, circled them. The parents prayed. The children hid their faces in the folds of their father's garment. The lioness made her lunge, and carried away the small girl by the throat.

"Let's pause there, shall we? There's lots more of that sort of thing – thousands of these guys getting chomped or speared or burnt. And I know exactly what you're gonna say. This is the Romans' doing. Can't blame the victims, can you? But you see, the thing is, these people – the men, the women, the little ones – they're only there because of good old Jesus H. Christ. Now, I don't know about you, but that's not something I'd like on *my* conscience. I mean, just how many kids being eaten like that would it take for this whole enterprise you're planning to start looking, well, counterproductive, eh?

"But let's move on. Because, you see, it isn't long before your guys start dishing it out as well as taking it. In fact, they pretty soon begin to dish out a lot more than they take. Dish it out in spades. I'm giving you one case here, to begin with. Check out this lady. Hypatia, they call her."

The screen showed a serene woman reading from a papyrus scroll.

"This is one clever lady, the most important philosopher of her time. Lives in a town called Alexandria, just when the Christians — that's what your followers start calling themselves — are taking over as top dog. But she still has a soft spot for the old ways: Zeus, Athena, Apollo, that crowd. So along come a rabble of monks and zealots and fanatics and they do this…"

The image switched to show a mob attacking Hypatia, their faces contorted with rage and hatred. They tore her from her carriage, and as she pleaded for her life they sliced away her flesh with oyster shells, and then, her lips still moving, they burned what was left.

"*Tut*, and I say again, *tut*. And all because she liked to offer up a little incense to the wrong gods. But things really heat up from here. Let me zip through this."

And there were more scenes of horror and persecution and war, each more terrible than the last. Christian armies converted pagans by the sword. Crusaders in clanking armour pillaged, raped and torched their way through the Jerusalem they had come to redeem. The great cities of Muslim Spain were left desolate. Everywhere: blood, fire and the burnt-out death of fire, and the bodies of children, and the cries of carrion birds circling.

"And the Jews, the Jews. You should see what they do to

the Jews. Two thousand years of persecution. What kind of legacy is that for a nice Jewish boy like you?"

Jesus bowed his head and mumbled a prayer.

"But this is only the beginning. The really good stuff isn't done by your guys to the other lot, pagans, unbelievers, whatever. No, the fun really gets going when the Christians start tearing each other apart. You know this as well as I do – real hatred is between brothers."

More pictures of war followed. Massacres of Catholics by Protestants; of Protestants by Catholics.

The eyes of Jesus burned but he could not look away.

"I reckon we've seen enough of that, don't you? Now there's just one last thing I want to show you."

The blank window filled with an image of the night, or so it first appeared. Millions of tiny lights glittered against a blue-black sky. And then the camera began to zoom in. The millions became thousands, and the thousands became hundreds. The dots of light took on a troubling complexity until just a few filled the screen. They were not stars, not these, and Jesus felt his stomach knot in revulsion.

"We've got a smell function here, if I can find the right button." The nail tapping at the remote was now oddly hooked and thick and grimy.

A smell drifted through the desert. The smell of scorching fat and the acrid stink of burning hair.

And now just one figure, wreathed in flames, was visible. The woman's rags had burnt away, and her skin was blackened and her face was in a place beyond pain. No, not beyond pain, but at the furthest reaches of pain, and the only place beyond it is death.

"Popcorn?"

The man held out a bucket. Jesus knocked it from his hand, scattering the popcorn over the ground, where it turned again to pebbles and grit. For a second, the cheerful, inquisitive, businesslike face of the figure changed, and not even the mirrors fastened to the man's face could conceal the red fire in his eyes. And then the fire was hidden again.

"Yeah, sure, you got upset," he said. "Only to be expected. Who's the woman? You wanna know who she is? Does it matter? Pagan, heretic, witch, who cares? My point is, she's burning – hell, they're all burning – because of you. Because of what you teach. Because of what it makes men do. But you can stop it. Just walk away. Give it all the finger. The disciples, the water into wine shtick, the lepers, the woman who washes your feet with her hair, the guy you bring back from the dead, the scourging, the crown of thorns, the death on the tree, the whole lot. Say the word and it's gone. Quite literally never happens. And when that goes, everything else goes too. No persecutions, no crusades, no burning babes like this one here. We're all laughing."

Jesus stared into the desert and saw an unexpected last brilliant flaming of red ochre before the darkness came.

"Let's get it on paper, shall we? Not that I wouldn't take your word, but it's good to have these things on file. No need

to read the small print; it's just the usual stuff for the law-
yers – you know what they're like. Just sign here. In blood.
No, only kidding. It's not like we're a couple of spindly goths
hanging round a graveyard in Sheffield. Ink's fine. Use this.
Just click on the top there and it … you got it. *Thaaaaat's*
great. OK, OK. Give you a lift back into town? No? Suit
yourself."

And then Satan was gone, leaving Jesus alone on the
bleak mountainside with the darkness upon him. And the
screen was just the stars in the night sky, and the soft seat
was a flat rock.

And Jesus thought about the smile on the face of Satan
as he left and the truth came to him at last, and he allowed
himself a glimpse of the future as it now stood. He saw
what would become of the world. Saw that the evil was now
greater. Saw that what had been small points of flame was
now one great conflagration.

And then, not knowing whether to go up to the mountain top, where still a little light might be found, or down
into the endless black of the valley, he cast himself onto the
stony ground.

And Jesus wept.

THE BURNING GLASS

Marcus Sedgwick

In May 1814, following his abdication, the former Emperor of France Napoleon Bonaparte was exiled by the allied governments to the Mediterranean island of Elba.

n the Musée des Arts et Métiers in Paris there are some extraordinary machines from across the ages of scientific invention. Here hangs Foucault's famous Pendulum, whose gentle swings disclose the rotation of the earth, and here also sits another of his great inventions: a multiple contraption comprising a large wooden table under which rests an enormous pair of bellows. On top of the table there are various clamps and tubes of brass construction. There is a tuning fork, a series of seven small round mirrors on spindles, and a small lens able to spin freely and at great speed. There is something a bee-keeper would recognize as a smoke generator. With this unlikely assortment of instruments, in 1862 Foucault determined the speed of light to within 0.6 per cent of its currently accepted value. Next to the machine is a larger but at first glance similar-looking apparatus. On the whole it seems a clumsy, unsophisticated ancestor of Foucault's cunning device, waiting in vain to evolve into something that actually works; but in fact its true function remains a mystery to this day.

A small brass plaque bears the name of its creator, an illustrious predecessor of Foucault's: Antoine Laurent Lavoisier.

December 1814. The one-time King of Italy, Mediator of the Swiss Confederation, Protector of the Confederation of the Rhine, First Consul of the French Republic, Emperor of the French, Napoleon Bonaparte, stood at the railing of the terrace, his hands clamped to the cold iron balustrade. He stared gloomily down across the grounds of the house, across the town, to where he could, if he stood on tiptoe, catch a glimpse of the bay, a knife of sullen water piercing the coast of Elba.

He tried to outstare the cold grey eye of the sea for a moment longer, then spun on his heel and stomped inside to his bedroom.

The sea. The irony was not lost on him. Apart from maybe that early glorious victory at Point L'Eguillete, he'd never been any good with the sea. To think he'd originally sought a naval commission! Thank God he'd studied artillery at the École in the end. Guns were simpler; you knew where you were with a gun: either it was pointed at you, or you were pointing it at someone else. Yes, the sea had dogged him always; it had always been there. Growing up on a small island had fixed that destiny for him, yet he had never understood the sea. And yes, the British fleet was unassailable, as it had been in Egypt, as it had been at Trafalgar. He banished the name as soon as it reared in his head, but he was left with the inevitable self-confession that his failures at sea were not only due to British ships, but the bald fact that he had always been useless at naval matters. He had long ago given up being angry at why, when his encyclopedic knowledge of and skill at warfare on land had secured the imperial title for him, his decisions at sea had always been ineffectual at best, contradictory and sui-cidal at worst.

Yes, the sea, the sea. And yet now, with a last twist of fate, it would be the sea that would bring him his salvation. Even now, somewhere out in the Mediterranean, that salva-tion would be approaching on a small sloop from Sicily.

It was getting dark; night would come and then there was the long emptiness to be got through. He glared at his bed in the corner of the fine room, the typical French bateau lit: another reminder of the sea. He would lie adrift there again through the small hours, gazing at the ceiling in the half-light, brooding, planning, plotting.

A tedious image of Mathilde, the slow-witted maid who performed general serving duties, flashed through his mind, and he decided to pour a large glass of Armagnac himself. It was foul weather, cold and damp, though at least it was not raining for once. He swilled the brandy around the glass, closed his eyes and inhaled the distilled sunshine that reminded him of happier days, of the vineyards of Corsica, of his youth, of girls he had caressed, then poured the fire of the drink down his throat, rang the bell to have supper in his room, and steeled himself for the clumsiness of Mathilde and the soup tureen.

It was a strange exile, he thought as he lay in a warm bath the next morning. Ever since the frozen hell of Moscow two years ago he'd been on the retreat, he could see that now, a series of defeats culminating in that drubbing at Leipzig. From there it had been just six months till the allied forces took Paris and days later forced his abdication. And yet, rather than the guillotine or some jail, he'd been sent to Elba, to rule over the tiny island just as he had once ruled over half the civilized world. Under the ever watchful eye of the British Commissioner, his powers were limited to an extent, but damn them! If they intend to humiliate me, he had thought, they will think again. *Alors*, I shall rule this Lilliput with pride and skill and I shall make the people love me!

Even before the Elbans knew he was coming, there'd been riots against French rule. Yet, when he'd stepped onto the quayside in May he'd won the crowd over in under an hour. Six months later and they loved him, yet even in this success there was danger, and Napoleon knew from his spies that his ultimate jailers, the allied powers, were planning a more permanent solution for him. There was some talk of exile to some remote British rock in the South Atlantic, while other informers whispered over a drink that his fate lay in a short drop with a rope around his neck.

Napoleon had laughed at that, and his spy had choked on his drink. "If they can't give me the honour of the guillotine," he said, "I won't give them the satisfaction of dangling for them." He fished inside his tunic and pulled out a small black taffeta bag held on a thin gold chain about his neck. "I've always had this with me, and if the time comes to use it, then use it I shall."

The spy had gawped at the bag, his thoughts racing at exactly what hideous poison lay within.

No, thought Napoleon, it was not exactly imprisonment to rule over twenty thousand peasants from a well-appointed house, with a stipend of two million francs, and with a court containing, among others, a treasurer, four chamberlains, a military governor, a doctor, a chemist, a butler, eight chefs, two valets, two equerries, twenty-seven stable hands, a director of music, two rather pretty singers, two washerwomen, a porter, footmen, and various young servants, even if one of them was the dreadful Mathilde. It was not jail, he knew that, for he had experienced true imprisonment: two weeks in the Chateau d'Antibes in the wake of Robespierre's downfall.

Thoughts of Robespierre begat memories of the days of blood, and his mind drifted back to the revolution. The revolution had given him everything. With the old order swept away, a man like him, with a decisive, military mind, had risen to the top so very easily. He took the revolution for what it was; he neither loved it nor hated it: he had used it.

And yet, as fortunes unwound and people's stars rose and fell, he had tasted the best of it and the worst. There had been so much death, so many men sent to the guillotine, and for what? For ideals? For noble causes? No! For treachery and fear. He saw things like no one else did, that many executions were so very pointless, but in those days, before he became First Consul, there was nothing he could do, except watch with the crowd as men made their way up the short flight of steps to the high, hanging blade. Men like the King himself, Louis; poets and writers like Chénier and de Gouges; men like Saint-Just and Robespierre and Danton, who had started the thing in the first place; and truly great men, like the genius scientist Lavoisier. Napoleon remembered what Lagrange, the mathematician, had said: "It took them only an instant to cut off that head, but France may not produce another like it in a century."

Too bad. There were many headless corpses in the cemeteries of Paris.

Napoleon Bonaparte rose from his steaming hot bath, an addiction he still fed, and pulled the bell rope. It would take at least five minutes for either of his ageing valets to make it from the servants' quarters up to his rooms, and he contemplated his naked self in the full-length mirror in his dressing room. It was not a superb sight, and the corners of his mouth turned down ever so slightly. It was true he had lost some weight recently, and for what he had in mind for his future, that was just as well. If he was to command loyalty and passion in his men once again, he would need to cut a dashing figure; and with his lack of height the last thing he could afford was to be overweight. Still, there was a way to go yet: a few months, perhaps; he would have to speak to the chef. He would need to spend more time riding. Then maybe he'd recapture the looks of his youth.

But, oh God, his hair was thinner than ever. Once, it had been long and flowing; now the remaining strands clung to his head like thin black cotton. He reached for the small green bottle of hair tonic and began to massage a good dollop into his scalp.

There was a brief tap at the door, and the elder of the valets crept into the room and, apparently unmoved by the corpulent nudity before him, began to lay out items of clothing for the former Emperor of the French. Napoleon ignored the man, but then was surprised to realize that the old stone was actually speaking to him.

"Your Imperial Majesty, I am to inform you that we have received word that your visitor will be arriving tonight."

"What? What? So soon?"

"Yes, sir. This evening. Shall it please your majesty to receive the monsieur for dinner?"

Napoleon spoke to the room, not to the man. "Indeed. It shall. It shall please me very much."

"Very good, sir. And may I inform the footmen and the butler of the gentleman's name?"

"No," hissed Napoleon. "You may not."

"Sir?"

"He has no name here. Do you understand me? No name."

The old valet nodded. He knew better than to do anything other than back out of the room, still nodding, bowing as low as his old bones would let him.

No name, though in Napoleon's mind the monsieur had only one name: Salvation.

But as the day passed, it looked unlikely that Monsieur Salvation would arrive that evening, as the weather turned up a petulant storm that threatened to keep all but the largest ships at bay.

Napoleon sulked. He'd lost interest in Elba already. It was a rock in the Mediterranean, of little consequence, not a major trading post as he'd been led to believe. The people might love him but they refused to pay their taxes; his retinue, his Lilliputian court and his guardsmen were costing him a fortune; and there was no sign of his two million francs from "King" Louis. The allies had set up the

puppet king to rule in his place; surely the fop wouldn't have
the nerve to go against British orders and not pay Napoleon
his money? To think he'd left lands worth a hundred and
sixty million francs to come to this crap hole!

In a fug of unhappiness he did what he always did
these days and called for his doctor, the treasurer, the
grand marshal of the palace, and a pack of cards. They
played vingt-et-un all morning. Napoleon cheated ter-
ribly, everyone pretended not to notice, he lost anyway,
and then sulked even worse.

"Pah!" he exclaimed, turning the elegant card table
upside down with one swing of his left riding boot. Three
pairs of eyes rolled in their sockets and then watched the
retreating back of the "Emperor", who stole off into the
depths of the house.

"He needs a woman," declared the grand marshal, pick-
ing up cards.

"He's had too many of those," said the treasurer, thinking
of the expense.

"What he needs," said the doctor, "is a war."

The other two looked at him, slightly appalled.

"It's all he knows how to do well," the doctor said,
shrugging to excuse himself. It wasn't *his* fault the man
was a maniac.

Napoleon's way led him blind into the domestic quarters of
the servants, where he joylessly pinched the bottom of the

prettiest chambermaid, who screamed because she knew she was expected to, not because she felt like it, and then he found himself standing in the kitchens. It was mid-morning; there was no one around, but various ingredients for the day's meals lay at hand: fresh bread from the market, some jugs of milk still warm from whatever fetid cow had been assaulted that morning, some palm-sized fish that from their smell were not as fresh as the fishmonger had claimed, eggs and fruit and vegetables. He smiled, then, hearing someone coming, slipped something into his pocket and stole out into the courtyard, wiping the smile from his face.

He hurried through the rain and into the house by the main entrance, sweeping up the steps.

"Bertrand!" he called. "Bertrand! Where is that man?"

Footmen began scurrying around, and within minutes Napoleon's most loyal aide, the Comte Henri-Gratien Bertrand, was hurrying down from his room.

"Sir?" he said, brushing his greying hair back over his head with a furtive gesture and tucking his shirt tails in.

Napoleon seemed not to know or care. "Walk with me, Henri," he said. "My heart is heavy. All this waiting – I cannot bear this inaction! It is death."

Napoleon threw a brotherly arm round Bertrand's shoulder, an unfamiliar gesture on his part, but Bertrand knew better than to question anything. They walked around the house twice and then turned into the drawing room, where the doctor and his friends were still playing cards.

"Ah, gentlemen!" Napoleon declared as they came up to watch the game. "Bertrand and I were just discussing this awful weather. I fear it will last all week, but Bertrand assures me it will pass by this evening. What do you think?"

"Oh," said the treasurer, a dimwit, and even shorter than Napoleon. "Well, I … that is…"

"It may continue," pronounced the grand marshal with great deliberation, "or then again, it may not."

The doctor sighed.

"Quite so, quite so," said Napoleon, "but whatever, this atmosphere has given me dreadful rheum."

The doctor sighed even louder. "Dreadful *what*?" he asked.

"Rheum! My nose. Sniffles and what all. And I have come down without a kerchief. Bertrand, lend me yours, will you?"

"Hmm, yes, of course," said Bertrand, who, rummaging in his pocket, pulled out not only a crumpled handkerchief, but a small smelly fish that fell neatly onto the middle of the card table.

Napoleon began to make strange strangled snuffling sounds, which is what he did to show he was laughing. The doctor sighed, the grand marshal rolled his eyes, and only Bertrand had the sense to start laughing too.

"Oh, very good, sir," he said. "Very funny. Indeed."

It wasn't quite enough, and Napoleon stomped away again in a worse mood than ever.

"Bloody, bloody hell," said Bertrand. 'What are we going

to do? That man once ruled half the known world…"

"Perhaps," said the doctor, as if he knew more than he did, "this mysterious visitor will lift his spirits?"

Bertrand turned to the rain-lashed window. "Perhaps. If he ever gets here."

"Who is he anyway?"

"I don't know. Napoleon refers to him only as 'L'."

"What kind of bloody name is that?"

Bertrand almost smiled. "It's the name of someone who doesn't exist."

But that evening, the rain suddenly vanished as if by an act of God, and the stars were reflected on the bay, which was as calm as a bird bath. Napoleon stood at his window, gazing out into the darkness, when the elder valet appeared.

"He will be here tonight, sir. But rather late."

"Very well, very well. Get them to put out a cold supper. Light a fire. And then everyone can go to bed."

He said it as if he were saying "Go to hell", but the valet merely bowed, grateful for the rest of the evening off.

Two hours later, the Emperor of Elba sat in near darkness in the long dining room, at one head of the table. Before him a place was set, matched at the far end of the table. Between the two plates lay fifteen feet of cold cuts, jellies, egg dishes, cheeses, breads, wine and water.

He was thinking about his women. His wives, Joséphine

and Marie Louise, now both gone; and Marie Walewska, his Polish mistress, perhaps the only one who'd ever really loved him.

There was a tap at the door. A footman opened it without waiting to be called, and then ducked out of sight, leaving a tall caped figure standing in the shadows of the doorway.

Napoleon rose slowly to his feet. "So," he said. "It is true." Then a doubt crossed his mind. "I cannot see you there. Come in. Come and sit down."

The figure moved into the room, automatically closing the door behind him. Napoleon noticed the action. Good! This is a man with a cautious mind, he thought.

The figure moved slowly down the room, passing the five-sticked candelabra in the middle of the table, giving the Emperor a chance to see if he'd been fooled. He made a quick calculation in his head. My God! Had it been twenty years? That would make him...

"Seventy? No! Seventy-one."

The figure stopped in its slow progress along the length of the room. "Correct."

His voice was as Napoleon remembered, precise and economic, though you could hear the extra years in it now.

"Please," Napoleon said, not a word he had much use for, "please, sit down."

"Thank you, I shall, for I am an old man."

"You were old when they killed you."

"Only six years older than you are now. Does that feel old

to you?" There was bitterness in the man's voice; anger at the waste. "I was at my prime. Not physically. But my work, my great work, was just beginning."

Napoleon felt a shiver travel down his spine. "Lavoisier," he breathed, "it is truly you."

"At your service."

"What did the judge say at your trial? The old fool! Something about 'We have no need—'"

"'—of genius.' Yes, I have heard those words in my mind every day. Every day, for twenty years, Napoleon. But here I am. And in all those twenty years, I never had the chance to thank you. I suppose I should."

Napoleon felt the remark cut him. "You suppose?" he said. "Most men would be grateful for their lives. Are you not?"

"For my life, yes. Thank you. But what kind of life is worth living? I have spent twenty years on the run; I have lived in sixteen different countries in that time. I have not put one foot in France since the day after my 'execution'. Your man smuggled me to the coast, to England first. It was clear I could not stay there long. Then to Ireland. My God! What an awful wet place that was. Two years! Then back to the Continent, always moving when the rumours started again, heading into more and more remote regions. And my work! Once, I had three laboratories in Paris. For these twenty years I have dragged my laboratory behind me in horse and cart, through the mud and snows of Europe.

What have I done in that time, apart from spend the fortune you sent me away with? Almost nothing! So, my Emperor, you will forgive me if sometimes I wish that I had died under the guillotine that day, instead of that poor stooge you disguised as me."

He fell silent, the rapid fire of his speech having spent itself, and coughed gently into an old silk handkerchief.

Napoleon sat open-mouthed; he was not used to being spoken to in this way. Even during the retreat from Moscow, not one of his generals would have dared be so bold.

"Did I force you to live?" he asked quietly, fingering the chain of the small black bag at his neck. "I suppose in a way I did, for who can really take their own life? But what could I have done? I was not Emperor then. I was a general with money and some power. It was as much as I could do to save a man whose skills I knew France could not afford to lose. I got you out. I gave you money. And then I never heard from you again. For five years I had my spies hunt for you. I needed you! But you were nowhere. I became Emperor and my dominions covered almost every country in Europe. But even in those ... other countries, Britain and Russia, I had my spies. And no one could find you. After ten years I believed you were dead. How could I have helped you then?"

"And excuse me," he continued, waving a hand at the darkened room, "but as you see, life has been difficult lately. I was betrayed! By fortune and the stupidity of my generals.

I chased from one end of Europe to the other, doing what no one could do but me: Egypt, Spain, Italy, Austria, Poland. And then came Russia and the bloody Czar. He needed to be taught a lesson, and by God, I intended to. The largest army ever to walk the earth! Half a million men, Lavoisier, can you imagine? Half a million men walked into Russia and I won. *I won.* We took Moscow, Alexander scurried around like the idiot he is, and yet it all came to nothing. I was defeated in the end, but not by Russia. By the weather. The winter!

"My God, Lavoisier, you have never seen anything like that. You, the great scientist! In all your wanderings around Europe, you never saw what I saw in Russia in 1812. We captured Moscow, and then? What? I didn't have the men to hold it, and I ... may have hesitated. We pulled out of the city, putting it to the torch, only to find the Czar's men coming at us from the south. We engaged, it was bloody, and then we began the long walk out of Russia, but the winter beat us to it. And the cold... Holy Christ, the cold. The snows came early, they said, and caught us while we were still halfway to Vilna. The temperature dropped and kept dropping. Forty below zero! For three weeks.

"You have never seen anything like that, Lavoisier, with all your science. You should have been there, to learn what the cold will do to a man who tries to keep walking until he freezes on his feet. There were those who made the mistake of taking their boots off; they would never get them back

on again, and frostbite took their toes in days. There were
those who lay down in the cold and went to sleep; but the
ones who kept walking were worse. Their faces! Their faces
were red, flushed with blood, as if their veins had frozen and
blocked, but still they walked until their noses and ears bled.
I saw tears of blood, Lavoisier – is such a thing possible?
Yes, I saw it. And still they would walk until they froze where
they stood. And if they made it to the bivouac each evening,
still they were not safe. I saw men walk straight into a camp-
fire and lie down, oblivious to the fact they were burning to
death. And no one tried to stop them. There was precious
little firewood to be had…"

He stopped, the force of his vitriol seeping away among
the awful memories.

"And then, just before they sent me to this prison island,
one of my spies heard an interesting story about a scientist
in England who had a trace of a French accent…"

Lavoisier inclined his head slightly. He didn't mind the
Emperor's rantings. He knew him of old, and he had of
course heard of his developments.

"*Et voilà!* Your servant, ready to do your bidding."

"At a price."

"Naturally."

Napoleon thumped the table. "Dammit! This is France
we're talking about."

"No, it isn't," Lavoisier said. "It's you we're talking about."

Napoleon stood. "We'll talk more tomorrow. I am going

to bed. A room has been prepared for you. Eat something if you will."

Lavoisier stood. "Thank you, no. I am not hungry."

Over breakfast two days later, the two men met again. Lavoisier had spent his time supervising the transportation of what passed for his laboratory from the docks up to the house. Napoleon had turned over an unused kitchen to the stranger, with the strictest instructions that no one was to enter the room or disturb him in any way.

"What is it that you want?" Lavoisier asked, though he had more than a rough idea.

Napoleon regarded the face opposite him. Now impossibly wrinkled, its characteristic almond shape, long nose and wide eyes were still the same as ever, though there was a touch of death in those eyes that had not been there before. Lavoisier, for his part, was studying the eyes of the Emperor, thinking that even when he smiled, there was always the look of death about him.

"When I knew you first," Napoleon said, "I was a student at the École. You were ending your time at the Royal Gunpowder Administration. Was it 1787? The accident?"

"It was 1788," Lavoisier said testily.

"What happened? I heard you were experimenting with some new explosives."

Lavoisier said nothing.

"They must have been … efficacious. Mademoiselle

Chevraud was killed in the explosion, was she not?"

Lavoisier had been goaded enough. "Yes," he spluttered. "And that fool Le Tors. He would never listen to my instructions. And yes, it was a new gunpowder I had developed. Lethal. It was absolutely lethal, very unstable at the time. I had struck on using a different potassium salt than is usually used. The nitrate of potassium is the usual component of gunpowder, but I was using potassium muriate. Twice as powerful. I believe it liberates more oxygen in the combustion process, and as my early work on oxygen proved, this gas is—"

"Yes, yes, very well," snapped Napoleon. "I know you can kill people. My question to you is this. Can you manufacture it again? Could you make, for example, enough for two hundred thousand men?"

Lavoisier smiled. "Give me a place to stand, and I will move the earth. Of course I can, given enough time, and money, but you have a garrison here of what? Five hundred men? What do you want with such large amounts of gunpowder?"

"Six hundred," said Napoleon pedantically, "but the weaponry is not for Elba. Come with me."

He stood and walked over to a small door that led off the side of the dining room. Lavoisier followed the Emperor along ornate corridors and up narrow stairs to a small study on the first floor. Napoleon fiddled with the blinds, trying to shed a little more light into the room, in the centre of which stood a large square table, the entire surface of which was covered with a detailed map of Europe.

"The best my map-makers ever made," he said proudly. "Come and look, come and look."

They wandered around the map, admiring its beautiful draughtsmanship, its colour and detail.

Lavoisier gazed at the map, almost speechless. A tear formed in one eye. "How much of it I saw! But how much still to see!" His hand stroked the outline of the French coast.

"You will see France again," Napoleon said, as if soothing a child. His eyes scoured the map greedily. "In the spring we will leave this rock, you and I, and as many men as I can muster from Elba, from Sicily, from Corsica. We will land on the French coast, somewhere near Antibes, and then we will strike inland. We will march this way, through the Bas Alps, to Grenoble, thence to Rives and Lyons. Then Paris. We will arrive there without firing a shot. Undoubtedly on the way we will meet some force sent to intercept us, and I will throw my coat open and say, 'Here is your Emperor's breast. Kill me if you will! If not, follow me to glory!' and the men will all fall on their knees and shout, '*Vive L'Empereur!*' They will love me as they did before and we will depose the puppet king. Then the British and the Russians will start to fear me, and will send forces to engage me.

"Most likely I will march north-east to Brussels, and battle will be met." He pointed at the map idly, his finger drifting, his mind playing out the military encounters like a game of chess. "Maybe here, at Wavre, or Mont-Saint-Jean, or at some godforsaken village near by, like this one, Waterloo."

"You dream!" Lavoisier said.

"No, I know these things. This is my world and I will win these battles, with the help of your world. You will make enough of this gunpowder of yours to blow the British into the sea!"

"No," said Lavoisier simply, "I won't."

"You will."

"No," Lavoisier repeated, "I won't. As it happens, I have already sold the recipe to the British."

"What!" roared Napoleon. He thundered round the table and roared at Lavoisier again. "Treachery?"

The old man held up a hand. He was not in the business of winning arguments by shouting. Napoleon fell silent.

"I had to make some money somehow. I ran out of what you gave me ten years ago. Anyway, the gunpowder is lethal. Impressive in a demonstration, maybe, but impractical in the field. Now, keep your peace and come with me. It is my turn to show you something."

The old scientist led the way down through the bowels of the house to his improvised laboratory, where he swung the door aside to allow the Emperor in. Napoleon was still on the edge of anger, but he was impressed nonetheless.

"You have been busy," he remarked, gazing at the apparatus that cluttered every surface and most of the floor.

Lavoisier shrugged. "This was why you kept me alive, was it not? So that this would not be lost. Let me show you something." He fumbled through a sheaf of papers clumsily, until he found what he was looking through, and handed it to Napoleon. "Did you ever see this?"

"Never. What is it?"

"It is a machine I designed, built and tested, forty years ago. It is called the Burning Glass."

The drawing showed a flat wooden wagon, thirty feet long, upon one end of which was mounted a huge circular glass object, a lens. It rested between two hefty metal screws which seemed intended to facilitate vertical movement. Ten feet away, and again on an adjustable track, was a smaller lens, but still perhaps four feet across. Various other handles and levers were fixed here and there.

"What does it do?"

"It annihilates things. It incinerates them, using the rays of the sun. It makes them catch fire, sometimes even explode."

Napoleon was impressed, but Lavoisier waved his hand.

"In practical terms it is useless as a weapon, unless you can contrive to get your enemy to place his head on the focus block here. Then you could fry his brains, but only an enemy with no brains at all would be stupid enough to get so close. Not only that, but it is cumbersome: very, very heavy and hard to manoeuvre. Can you imagine that

in the mud of the battlefield? We abandoned it for anything other than scientific use."

"So why show it to me?"

"I am trying to educate you, to teach you something of
the methods of the natural philosopher, to show you the
agonizingly slow steps he takes towards his goal."

"Show me the goal," said Napoleon.

Lavoisier sighed. "Very well."

He turned to the table behind him, and with a flourish
more befitting a magician than a scientist, whipped a cover-
ing cloth away to reveal a board six feet long, upon which
stood an array of mirrors and lenses, all securely bolted to
the base, but all free to pivot vertically.

"This…" Lavoisier said, then stopped. He glanced out
of the kitchen window. "For a man such as yourself, it will
be easier to show you. Here, you will have to help me with
this. I cannot lift it. Call someone, but someone you can
trust."

Napoleon nodded and turned to the kitchen steps.
"Bertrand!"

The Burning Glass stood on a small table in the courtyard.
Bertrand kept asking questions but Napoleon ignored him,
occasionally waving him back a few feet. The Emperor
himself hovered at Lavoisier's shoulder, while the old man
fiddled and adjusted and calibrated and estimated.

"Very well," Lavoisier said finally. "It is not perhaps as

perfect as I would like it, but not bad after six months at sea. Very well. So, you will observe that today is a sunny day. A winter's day, but the sun is shining, yes? Now…" He gazed around the courtyard. "Behold the lemon tree over there. If you please."

Napoleon and Bertrand did as they were told and turned to watch the innocent little tree growing at the far side of the three-sided courtyard. Beyond, the land fell away from the house, down to the town, down to the sea. Lavoisier made one last adjustment, then flicked a mirror so that it faced the sun directly. Instantly a focused ray of brilliant white light shot across the courtyard, where it struck the tree, which after four or five seconds of smouldering burst into flames.

A heavenly citrus scent wafted across on the gentle breeze. Napoleon's nostrils twitched, and he knew it was the smell of victory.

"How far can that thing reach?" he said quietly.

"Effectively? A kilometre. And," Lavoisier said, slowly and slyly, "just think the effect it will have on the powder magazines of the English, that new and highly volatile gunpowder that I showed the English how to make."

Napoleon turned to Lavoisier and, without saying a word, kissed him on either cheek.

"There is one note of caution. This device requires a clear sight of the sun. No sun, no beam of light. Understand?"

Surely even the Emperor would grasp that fact.

AUTHOR'S NOTE: It all came true, just as Napoleon had predicted. He sailed for France and arrived in Paris on 20 March, his son's birthday, without firing a shot, just as he foretold. The night before, Louis XVIII panicked and fled the city. By June the Grande Armée was reborn, and engaged the British forces commanded by Wellington at Waterloo.

Everything was as the Emperor had declared it would be, with one exception.

It rained.

VIENNA, 1912

Mal Peet

MAY

I watch him beating carpets, and it breaks my heart. I stand at our thin window and look down into the courtyard and watch him beating Frau Metzner's carpets and it just breaks my heart. He's hung them on a rope he's stretched between the back-entry gate and a hook set into the wall. He's hitting them with an English cricket bat that he got from God knows where. Every whack brings forth a cloud of dust and he steps back out of it, coughing. He shouldn't have to be doing it. He's an artist. And he isn't strong.

The two Metzner brats are watching Addie from the corner of the yard, giggling at him. Their stupid little dog yaps every time the bat bangs against the carpet. Their mother will pay Addie a measly fifty groschen for his morning's work, and without saying anything he'll go and buy bread and sausage and a paper twist of tea, even though he needs paints. He's painting autumn landscapes now because he's almost run out of green.

The living room is also Addie's studio. He paints at the

little table, on old door panels usually, canvas when we can afford it, propped against the wall. It's bad for his back, working like that. And the light from the small window isn't good enough. It suffocates his colours, he says. Suffocation is a word Addie uses a lot. It's one of the bees in his bonnet. He has lots of bees in his bonnet. It's a hive.

"This isn't a living room," he'll cry. "It's a dying room! It's crushing me!"

It's very small, it's true. And it's the kitchen as well. When there's washing drying by the fire there's hardly room to move. But it's all we can afford.

"I need space," he says. "Space! Room to breathe! To create!"

That's why he paints landscapes, I think. Big open spaces he can go into. It's terrible for him that he has to paint them so small.

I used to ask him to paint me. I liked the idea of posing for him, of his eyes fixed on me. He has wonderful eyes, Addie. I once told him that he could be a stage hypnotist, like Mesmer. He smiled at that, and said, "Well, if I don't make it as an artist perhaps I'll give it a go." He did try to paint me, once. I wore my blue dress and sat in the chair holding a book. After a long time I said, "Can I see?" And instead he let out this terrible groan and slashed black paint all over the picture.

He'll never marry me. I'd like to be the mother of his children, but I know I won't.

JUNE

Just when things were getting really desperate, Addie came home with money. Eleven whole schillings! And a bag containing a meat pie, potatoes and cabbage and five tubes of paint. Also a bottle of Riesling, which worried me a little because drink doesn't agree with him. He was in a strange mood. Happy, because of the money and the paint, but also agitated. The work had come through his friend Werner the carter. Werner's usual man had been taken sick, so he'd asked Addie to help him with a job. Which was clearing the house of a widow who had died, on Lindaustrasse. A Jewish lady.

I peeled the potatoes and chopped the cabbage while Addie sat on the chair and brooded. His silences have a darkness to them, so after a while I managed to get him talking about the job.

He said, "Werner had the keys to the house and when we went in I couldn't believe my eyes. The hallway, the *hallway*, was bigger than this flat. The damned old Jewish bourgeoise had more room to park her umbrellas than we have to live in. Can you imagine that? Then there were two more floors and an attic and a cellar. She'd lived alone in all that space for more than fifteen years. The attic had windows that were full of light. Sucked in light. She'd kept a servant up there. I thought, I would die for such a space to paint in."

I said, "Light the lamp, Addie."

But he didn't. He swigged some wine and pulled a face, swallowing it. The room grew darker.

He said, "All the quality stuff had already gone, of course. The furniture and everything. There were pale patches on the walls where paintings had been. I wondered if they'd been any good. Probably not. People like that, what do they know about art? Anyway, we filled the cart with what looked like dreck to me, but Werner was pleased enough. We drove it all to a dealer Werner does business with. Another Jew."

Addie has a bit of a thing about Jews. A bee.

"The old rogue offered Werner thirty schillings for the lot. Werner laughed in his face. Then they argued the toss back and forth for what felt like an hour, the Yid waving his arms about and moaning that Werner was taking the food from his children's mouths and so on. In the end he coughed up forty-two schillings like he was parting with a pound of his flesh. Werner gave me twenty, which was bloody decent of him, I thought."

"He's a good man," I said.

Addie nodded. Then he stood up. "I'm going down to the baths," he said. "I feel dirty."

Addie has a thing about hygiene, too.

On Sundays, if the weather is good, Addie takes his paintings and his little postcard sketches to the Volksgarten. He hangs his paintings from the railings, like lots of other artists. He leaves the flat early, because there is always competition for the best places. Sometimes I go with him. I did today. Spring was turning into summer, and I knew that the flowers in the park would be opening to the sun and the trees would be dressed in fresh new shades of green. It would have been a perfect day if Addie had sold something.

There were so many people taking their afternoon stroll! And so many carriages that the boulevard was a rocking sea of horses' heads. The whole length of the railings alongside the park was hung with pictures, like a mad carpet. That's the trouble, of course. Addie's thoughtful little paintings get lost among the lurid sunsets, the garish portraits, the sentimental pictures of dewy-eyed dogs and children in frilly frocks. He needs to paint on big canvases. Huge canvases. But he sits there on his little folding stool, too proud to ask for recognition. It breaks my heart.

A man walking alone stopped and peered at one of Addie's pictures. One of my favourites. It's a house perched on the edge of a precipice. It looks as though it might fall in, but somehow you know that it won't, that it has the strength to cling on for ever. You see it in the distance, through the trunks of trees, as if you had made a long journey to reach it and feared that it might not be there. There is a light in one of the windows. The colours are mostly violet and ochre, because they were almost all that Addie had left when he painted it.

The man said, "Where did you paint this, Mein Herr?"

Addie doesn't usually give his pictures titles.

"In poverty," Addie said.

The man smiled. "So it is an imaginary scene?"

Addie looked down at his broken shoes. I was worried what he might say.

He said, "Of course. Everything that is truly good is imaginary."

The man nodded, as if he agreed. But then he leaned down and touched Addie on the shoulder. Addie flinched. He doesn't like to be touched.

The man said, "You paint well, but I happen to disagree with you. Imagination is highly suspect. Reality is what is beautiful. But we are blind to it because it is familiar. Don't you think it is the task, the duty, of the artist to make reality strange? To refresh the way we see it?"

Addie shrugged. He looked uncomfortable. He has strong views about art, and they differed from this man's. But he was reluctant to argue with a potential buyer.

He said, "The task of the artist is to pay the damned rent."

The man smiled again. "True. But the artist volunteers for other responsibilities, does he not? He shows his work and says, 'Here, see through new eyes.' For example, the trees in your painting are silver birches. But you have given their bark a lilac colour. Now, when I look at birches in the evening, I shall perhaps find that colour in them. Thus, you will have made a change in my way of seeing, which is a change to my life. A small one, perhaps, but a change nonetheless."

Addie, for the first time since I'd known him, was stuck for words.

He was saved by a commotion. An outbreak of shouting and cheering, a crush of people onto the pavement. I
was shoved back against the railings by the throng and I
only just managed to save my hat. A troop of the Imperial
Cavalry had clattered onto the Heldenplatz. My view was
blocked by the press of bodies. All I could see, in glimpses
between heads and shoulders, was the faces of the troopers,
stern and identical below the peaks of their crested hel-
mets, the pennants flying from their lances, the heads of
their horses tossing. I found it hard to breathe. Not because
of the crowding. It was as if the air had all been sucked
away, as if the people all around had inhaled at once and
left nothing for me. I could feel their excitement drowning
me as real as water.

There is a desire for war, which I share but do not understand.

Addie had climbed onto his little stool so as to see over
the crowd. He won't admit it, but he is shorter than I am. I
looked up at his face and saw the thrill in it. His blue eyes
bright as stars.

When the cavalry had passed by, the man who had perhaps considered buying Addie's painting had disappeared.

"Where'd he go?" I said.

"Who?"

"That man. The one who liked your painting."

Addie looked at me as though I was speaking a foreign
language.

He shrugged. "To hell with him," he said. "Did you see the Imperials? Weren't they magnificent?"

JULY

Werner's twenty schillings didn't last long. By the end of June we were hard up once again. Addie couldn't find much work. Besides, he's been spending more and more time at meetings of what he calls "the group". When he comes home he spends hours, sometimes half the night, writing furiously in the cheap notebooks he used to do sketches in. When he's writing he talks and argues with himself as if I'm not there.

I'm sure that he is a genius. I'm sure that one day he will be really famous. But, in the meantime, we have to eat.

So, two days ago, in the afternoon, while Addie was out, I tidied myself up a bit and went down to the cafe quarter. A man propositioned me and I went with him into the little alleyway behind Schwartzer's. With the money he gave me I bought a thick slice of pork belly and some potatoes. I came home and was peeling the spuds when someone knocked on the door. The only person who knocks on our door is the landlord when he wants the rent. I stayed silent, hoping he would go away, but I knew he wouldn't. So I dried my hands and arranged my face and opened up.

It wasn't the landlord. It was a smiling man in a beautiful pale grey suit. I was so surprised I couldn't speak. He took his hat off and I saw that it was the man from the park, the one who had talked to Addie about his picture before the cavalry came by and I'd lost my breath.

He didn't seem to recognize me, though, because he said, "I was told that Herr Hitler lives here. Is that correct?"

I told him yes, it was, but that Addie wasn't in. He seemed very disappointed. It was awkward, this stranger standing there. I didn't know what else to say. Then the stairs began to creak and someone coughed, climbing up. The visitor looked over his shoulder. "Might I come in for a moment?"

I could hardly refuse, could I?

In our wretched little flat he was like a fallen angel or something. But he looked around as though he was pleased with everything. He went over to where Addie's finished or abandoned paintings were propped against the wall and leaned to study them. I had nothing to offer him. Nothing that he would have wanted, anyway.

He straightened up and took a little silver case from his waistcoat pocket. It flipped open as if by magic and he took out a card.

He gave it to me and said, "I should be grateful if you would give Herr Hitler my compliments and ask if he would be so kind as to call upon me at this address. Any morning this week would be suitable. Or next week, if he is busy."

I nodded and said, "Thank you," which was stupid. He smiled.

At the door he turned. "Oh, and ask him if he would

bring with him his charming little landscape with the lilac birches. You know the one I mean?"

When Addie came home, I told him about the visit and gave him Doctor Solomon Etzmann's card. He looked at it for a whole minute.

"This man was *here*? A rich Jew was *here*? You let him in?"

"I didn't know he was a Jew, Addie. He was just the man who talked to you at the Volksgarten. He seemed very nice."

"God in heaven. What the hell did he want?"

NOVEMBER

He wanted to save us. He really was an angel. So much has happened! I hardly know where to start.

Addie refused to go at first. It took me almost a week to persuade him. He can be very stubborn. But poverty wins all arguments, as my mother used to say. So he went, and when he came back he was glowing.

"He bought the picture! Look!"

Addie put the banknotes on the table like a miracle. I think I cried, I can't remember. And then he told me that Doctor Etzmann had commissioned him – *commissioned* him! – to do a painting of his country house. Addie is really good at houses. Did I say that already? Anyway, Doctor Etzmann's house was near Waidhofen something-or-other. Addie had to wait until September, because that was when the trees had the best colour. That was all right, though, because the money for the birches painting kept us going until then.

So off Addie went with his palette and brushes as soon as the leaves started to turn. I thought he might ask me to go with him, but I suppose he decided I might be a distraction. He was gone a whole month. The money ran out – Addie had spent a lot of it on paint – and it was hard for me to make ends meet.

Anyway, he came back looking really well. A bit sunburned. And he'd put a bit of weight on, which suited him. Doctor Etzmann had really liked the painting, and had invited his neighbours to look at it, and three of them had asked Addie to paint their houses, too. Herr Steiner's in the spring, and Herr Popper's and someone else's in the summer. But they'd all given Addie what he called "a retainer", and Herr Steiner had bought a small landscape, so we had lots of money!

The best thing is that we have a nice new place to live. Addie told Doctor Etzmann that his eyes were failing in the shit hole (he actually used those words) we were living in. And, within a month, Doctor Sol (which is what I call him now, because it makes him laugh) had found us an apartment in the artisan quarter. The stairs are a bit of a climb, but it's worth it because one of the rooms has a huge north-facing window and the light pours in through it. And when I lug the shopping up, the first thing I see is Addie at his easel turning that light into the special things that only he can see.

* * *

At the end of October Doctor Sol invited us to his daughter's wedding. Addie was reluctant, at first. Despite everything, he still has a little grumble, just now and again, about "filthy rich Semites". We were nervous too, of course. Neither of us had been to a Jewish wedding before, and we didn't know what to expect. And it was a bit strange, what with the men and the women separated most of the time. Late in the afternoon, Rachel, Doctor Sol's other daughter, and I were going to the lavatory. She giggled and pulled me towards a pair of doors that weren't quite closed. Frantic music poured through the crack. I peeped in, and there was Addie, dancing with his arms around bearded men. He had a little round cap on his head, and he seemed really happy. Laughing. I realized I'd never seen him laugh before.

It nearly broke my heart.

EDITOR'S NOTE: Adolf Hitler moved to Vienna in February 1908, aged eighteen, in the hope of gaining a place at the Academy of Arts. After several unsuccessful attempts to make it as an artist, he left the capital in 1913. However, his six poverty-stricken years there had helped to formalize his anti-Semitism – views which would form the basis of his policy when he became Chancellor of Germany in 1933.

THE BLUE-EYED BOY

Linda Newbery

"Oi, Brett – shift yourself!"

The voice seemed to float towards him from a distance. Brett's eyes flickered open; it took a moment to remember where he was, why he was slumped against a hot window. The coach. He was on the coach. His mouth was open; he might even have been dribbling. The driver was slowing; they were entering a small town, a cluster of buildings around a brick church.

Joel already had his coat on, rucksack on his lap. "You were snoring!"

"Liar!"

"Wish I had earplugs."

Brett blinked himself properly awake as the coach pulled into a car park. Mr Wade, head of history, was standing up front beside the driver's seat, holding the mike.

"OK, this is Messines. We'll spend an hour and a half here. We're having a tour of the church – remember I told you the crypt was used as an aid post in the war? Then you can look at the museum. Back on the coach by four, everyone – and don't forget it's a *church*. No loud voices, no running, no inappropriate behaviour. Trudi, no chewing. Get rid of it." He pointed to the bin bag by the exit.

Brett shrugged on his jacket and shouldered his rucksack, glancing up at the clumped-together church with its odd-shaped tower. The other places had been more like it: trenches, tunnels, that huge bomb crater. Mr Wade had told them to imagine themselves as young soldiers about to go over the top, and yeah, he really could. But *this…*

"Fierce fighting took place around here from the autumn of 1914 and all through the war," Mr Wade was saying. "And see Messines Ridge there? Not a spectacular height, but it gave the Germans a commanding position. We'll get a better view from the bell tower."

Brett clumped down the steps behind Trudi. He wasn't about to get excited at the thought of tramping round some dismal old church.

As the young priest left his lodgings, he wondered, as he wondered every morning, How long can it go on, this war? How much more can we take?

Winter would soon be here, the long dark days, and now the armies had dug themselves in as if no one expected to move far. Months ago, at the start, it had seemed the Germans would sweep right through Belgium, into France and down to Paris, but they'd halted here, brought up against the British and Belgian armies. Stalemate. But it had come at a terrible price.

Already the shelling had battered the town of Messines and the priest's beloved church. It grieved him, gave him a physical pain, to see it damaged, surely beyond repair. When the war is over, he thought, we must build anew: build an even more splendid church, to stand against brutality and suffering.

And, now that the Germans had taken Messines, he was on the wrong side of the line. He could have fled, but Father Antonius said it was their duty to stay. They had to give help wherever it was needed. The farmers and their families couldn't leave; nor could the people in nearby villages. The young priest had travelled in Germany before the war and spoke the language, so had been sent by Father Antonius to comfort and pray with the wounded soldiers who straggled back from the front line.

Soldiers! Some of them were hardly more than boys. They hadn't chosen war, any more than the Belgians had, or the French, or the British. He prayed now as he walked, for these innocents caught up in the fighting, pitched against the deadly new machine guns that ripped flesh to pieces without even pausing for breath.

Now that the Germans had discovered the church crypt, they were using it as an aid post. The priest crossed himself as he approached the ruins and picked his way through the rubble of the cloisters. What would today bring? How many young men were up there on the ridge, healthy, full of vigour, who would tonight be groaning in hospital beds? Or, worse, lying in a makeshift morgue, awaiting burial? He shuddered. It seemed beyond human endurance.

God must have some purpose in this, the priest thought; he clung to that belief.

Down in the crypt, with its stone arches, the air struck cold. A morose group of Bavarian soldiers huddled there, drab and dirty in their field grey. Two sergeants – one on a camp bed, another shrouded in a blanket – were being tended by nurses, while the others waited. A young lance corporal, slightly built, dark-haired, sat on the steps, drawing in a sketchbook by the dim light from above. Only the man on the bed, who was groaning and barely conscious, seemed seriously injured. The nurses had only basic equipment: jugs of water, bowls, bandages, disinfectant.

The priest made his enquiries, expressed sympathy, offered help – though what could he do?

The elder of the two nurses seemed resentful of his intrusion. "They'll be moved back to the field hospital," she told him, "as soon as there's transport."

He nodded, understanding that space would be needed here for more casualties later in the day. He moved towards the young man on the steps, noticing a bloodstained bandage around one ankle.

"Good day, my friend," said the priest. "You do well to

occupy yourself, and take your mind away from your injury. May I see?" He leaned closer.

At first the lance corporal looked inclined to snatch his sketchbook out of view, but then, with a slight shrug, he offered it to the priest. In pencil, with a delicate touch, he had drawn the arches of the crypt, and the countess's grave.

"Very fine!" marvelled the priest. "Fine work indeed! Are you an artist in civilian life?"

"Yes. I am." There was something wary and guarded about this lance corporal. In his glance, shyness was mixed with arrogance.

"That's Leo, that is," said a corporal with a gashed head, wincing as the nurse dabbed at it none too gently. "You hardly see him without he's drawing something."

"Remarkable!" said the priest, handing back the sketch-book. "Well," he added to Leo, "I hope you'll soon be able to return to your artistic calling."

The young man nodded, and thanked him. The priest was struck by the steely blue of his eyes. A fire burned there, a longing. And the priest's heart filled with compassion for these young lads whose lives were being taken from them, to be gambled in this huge game of chance.

"And here," said the guide, "you see drawings and paintings by wounded German soldiers."

This wasn't Brett's idea of a museum – junk shop, more

like. Just a shabby collection of letters, bits of uniform, rusted grenades, ancient black and white photographs. The paintings weren't much either: fussy drawings and splodgy watercolours. Churches, graveyards, trees. The only one he liked was a drawing of a dog – flop-eared, rough-coated, bright-eyed. It reminded him of Bobby, his nan's fox terrier.

That night, in the hostel near Ypres, he sat with the other Year 10s for the daily writing-up of their journals. *We stopped at a church*, he began, and that was about all he could think of. He glanced across at Trudi, who was writing busily. Leaning across, he read: *The best bit was when Joel found the grave of his great-great-grandfather in the German cemetery.*

Yeah. He could put something about that. The grave of Gefreiter Samuel Goldstein, ranked among countless others like soldiers standing to attention, was the only one marked with a star.

"What's that for?" Brett had asked.

"It's a Star of David," Joel said. "To show he was Jewish."

"So are *you* Jewish then?"

"Course. Didn't you know?"

Brett shrugged. Didn't matter one way or the other.

"So you're German?" Trudi asked Joel.

"Half. My dad's family have lived in Berlin ever since eighteen hundred and something. They own a whole load of jewellery shops."

"Cool," said Trudi.

"So, wait." Brett was trying to keep up. "If we were in the war – like, *now* – you'd be on the other side?"

Joel grinned. "You got it. Faster than a speeding bullet."

Joel's great-great-grandad was killed in 1914, Brett wrote, and added, copying Trudi: *His name was Samuel Goldstein.*

Next day, returning to the crypt, the priest found no patients at all – just the two nurses, cleaning and tidying, making ready. High on the ridge, the guns had been rumbling since first light. It was bitterly cold. The priest wished the nurses good day, and asked after yesterday's casualties, the Bavarians. They'd been sent down to the field hospital, he was told. The younger nurse, the pretty fair-haired one, coloured up; he guessed she'd taken a fancy to one of the soldiers. It would be the blue-eyed boy with the intent gaze, he felt sure.

As he wasn't needed here, he decided to walk the three miles by road to the hospital, well back from the German line. Words of comfort and cheer, a prayer, might do the men some good. Sometimes he was called upon to deliver last rites, or hear a confession. But he did not reach the field hospital that day. Father Antonius intercepted him in the ruins of the town square and directed him to a nearby farm, where a local woman was dying from pneumonia.

Next day, he set off into the biting wind. The hospital was a cluster of tents, the ground much muddied. Someone was groaning horribly; another voice pleaded for morphine.

The sister, too busy to be interrupted, frowned and shook her head at the priest.

Then a man recognized him and called out; it was the corporal who had spoken to him in the crypt. His head and arm swathed in bandages, he propped himself up painfully in his truckle bed.

The priest hurried over. "How are you, my friend?"

"As well as can be expected," said the corporal with a grimace. "We lost Leo, though."

"What?"

"He died this morning."

"Died?" The priest was aghast. "But I thought his wound was only slight!"

"Sepsis, they said. Took hold very quickly."

The priest crossed himself, and prayed silently. Although he'd seen Leo only once, the thin face and yearning blue eyes had seared themselves into his memory.

"He started raving," the man went on. "Insisted on being moved away from the bloke in the next bed – reckoned he'd be contaminated. The nurses moved him along the tent just to give us all a bit of peace. Then they both died, anyway."

"It is God's will," said the priest.

The corporal nodded without much conviction. "He was a funny chap, Leo. Brave as a lion – rescued his officer last month, dragged him in under heavy fire, cool as you like. But he kept himself to himself. His drawings, though... He gave me one." He gestured towards his pack, which lay near by on the tarpaulin floor. "Have a look. That pocket there."

The priest unfastened the flap and took out the folded paper inside. It was a drawing of a dog – a flop-eared terrier, rough-coated, bright-eyed.

"Loved animals, Leo did," said the man. "That stray dog turned up near our lines. Foxy, Leo called it. Wouldn't be separated from it. Fed it from his own rations."

The priest looked at the pencilled signature. "So his name wasn't really Leo, then?"

"No!" The man laughed. "That was just my nickname for him. Leo, short for Leonardo. Our own little Leonardo da Vinci. Why don't you take it? You'll look after it better than I will."

In Ypres the three teachers were rounding up the Year 10s, who were investigating the marketplace's cafes, bars and chocolate shops. Chocolate could wait till tomorrow, Mr Wade insisted, shooing them along. Tonight they were heading for the Menin Gate, and the last post ceremony.

Arriving early, they had time to look at the Memorial to the Missing, a massive arch of brick and stone that spanned the road, each face carved with thousands and thousands of names.

Mr Wade gave the usual lecture about behaving respectfully during the short ceremony: no chewing, pushing, shoving or even talking. "It takes place at eight every evening, and it's a solemn occasion. Yes, Trudi, I know it's ancient history to you. But it's important to remember the World War. The War to End All Wars, people called it; and, well, there *have* been wars since, of course – Vietnam and Iraq to name just two – but none that involved as many countries as the World War. Not since the peace treaty of 1918."

A small crowd gathered by the arch; police on motorbikes stopped the traffic. Then uniformed buglers, three of them, sent out into the spring evening their plaintive notes, which seemed to lodge in Brett's chest, and wrench at him. Tears sprang from his eyes; he blinked them away before anyone saw.

It was over in minutes, then the crowd dispersed and the traffic flowed again.

"Is that *it*?" said one of the girls. "That's why we've come all this way?"

Mr Wade made himself tall and took a deep breath, ready to explain all over again.

Brett nudged Trudi and Joel. "Come on! Let's make a dash for it." If they were quick, they'd find a chocolate shop that was still open.

The funeral was conducted by an army padre. There were three to be buried, in simple wooden coffins, and only three other mourners besides the priest: the young nurse and two patients from the hospital, one on crutches. The corporal was too ill to attend. It was a brief, almost businesslike service. There were so many burials that this was a routine event. A chill wind cut in from the east, beneath a cloudy sky. Up on the ridge, the guns boomed. Prayers were said, responses mumbled. Tears coursed down the cheeks of the young nurse.

Afterwards the priest stayed by himself to meditate for a few moments on these three latest losses.

Gefreiter Samuel Goldstein.

Unteroffizier Heinz Schneider.

And Lance Corporal Leo.

Of course, his name was not really Leo, but the priest thought it suited him, with his slow-burning fierceness.

It was so heartbreakingly sad, the priest thought, to see the youth and strength of Europe sacrificed to the vast indifference of war. All the talents and potential of these young men, their futures, their children: thrown away, lost. He couldn't put faces to the other names, but to this last one he could. He recalled the brightness and passion of those blue eyes, the penetrating gaze. He'd seen pride there, single-mindedness, and driving ambition.

Standing by the graveside, head bent, he wondered what this man's destiny would have been had fate not dealt him such an early death. Who could tell how much had been lost? Who could guess what he might have achieved, in ten, or thirty, or fifty years' time, this Leo, this – to give him his real name – Adolf Hitler? He might have become a great artist; the whole world might have recognized his genius.

The workings of God, the priest reminded himself, cannot be known to mankind. We cannot begin to understand; we can only have faith.

As he walked away, he looked back at the three stark crosses, and rain started to fall.

AUTHOR'S NOTE: Lance Corporal Adolf Hitler was treated for an injury in the crypt of Messines Church, Belgium, in the winter of 1914. Shortly after this he was awarded the Iron Cross for bravery, for rescuing an officer under heavy fire. Hitler is known to have produced many drawings and paintings during his time as a soldier, one of which shows the ruined cloisters at Messines.

ECLIPSED

Matt Whyman

The nuclear stand-off between the United States of America and the Soviet Union, part of what was known as the cold war, dominated global politics for more than four decades after the end of World War Two. By the 1980s, people lived with the very real fear of a nuclear Armageddon...

I missed the moment that the moon exploded. Like so many people, I was fast asleep when it happened. According to my friend Maisie, whose neighbour works a night shift, it looked just like a mothball fragmenting into the void.

The morning after, I discovered my father staring out of the kitchen window. He was barely blinking. On the radio a news report claimed that America was demanding some explanation from the Soviets. At a time when the world lived in fear of a nuclear strike from one side or the other, it seemed like an act of madness for Russia to launch a lunar attack. My father didn't appear to be listening, however, and at first I didn't realize the enormity of what was being broadcast. It was only when I sneezed on account of my hay fever that he noticed me.

"Sleep well, cupcake?" he asked.

"Sure," I told him, looking around. "Where's Mum?"

As he pressed his lips into a smile, I noticed his eyes shine over. "She'll be back later," he said after a moment. "I promised her I'd tell you that."

At school I found everyone talking about the same thing. At first I thought I was the victim of a grand hoax. How could the moon just cease to exist? I had only been alive for fourteen years. Considering a lifetime without it seemed unthinkable. I remember that first day was clear and bright. The sky, as blue as a lagoon, had not a cloud in sight. During a special assembly, our headmistress explained that with the loss of the moon we faced a time of great uncertainty. Nobody knew for sure what effect its disappearance would have on everything, from the ebb and flow of the oceans' tides to the rate at which the earth revolved. Still, she assured us that nature would adapt and survive, as would mankind.

Throughout each lesson that followed, we kept turning our attention to the window. Even the teachers couldn't resist looking, despite the fact that there was nothing unusual to see.

Come dusk, as we made our way to our homes, stars began to prick the twilight. I kept looking up and around. I wasn't sure what I was hoping to spot. The moon might have sailed through every night sky for billions of years, but sometimes clouds, tall buildings or trees conspired to cover it up. Everything just looked so normal up there, so peaceful and serene.

I saw no smouldering remains or hole torn out of the heavens. Had I spent the day in my own company, without news or gossip, it would not have struck me that anything was different. Still, as an urgent breeze picked up all the litter in the streets, I couldn't help feeling that perhaps we had taken things for granted.

"Come and sit with us, cupcake. There's something we need to discuss."

I had found my parents facing one another at the kitchen table. Like everyone, they appeared a little shell-shocked and bewildered. They looked up when I came into the room. As soon as my father invited me to join them, I realized I had just killed a conversation.

"What's the latest on the moon?" I asked, noting the television switched on in the corner. The sound was muted, but the footage of the rockets climbing into the sky looked ominous.

"The moon?" My father paused and gazed at me. It left me feeling like I hadn't returned home in years. "I'm not sure," he said, and cleared his throat. "What did they tell you at school?"

I drew a chair from the table and sat with them. "The Russians are claiming a test firing went badly wrong. That's what our form teacher told us before the bell rang. They're suggesting the target coordinates were changed as an act of sabotage by the United States."

Mum clasped her mug with both hands. Not once did she take her eyes off it. "The last time I looked at the moon," she said, "it was on the wane."

I glanced at Dad, confused by her comment. "Mum," I said, "it isn't coming back."

Outside, the wind had strengthened so much that it began to moan and whistle. Only then did I notice that the curtains had been closed against the night sky. I looked at my dad, and found his focus upon me once again.

"This isn't about the moon," he said. "It's about us."

Until they told me Mum was moving out, I really hadn't known that my parents had been having problems. As it turned out, I don't think my dad had either. Sure, Mum would sometimes say that he loved his work more than he loved us, but we'd never taken her seriously. Looking back, I suppose this was her way of quietly convincing herself that the changes in her heart were for the best. I didn't cry when Mum revealed that she'd met someone else. I just nodded when she promised me that everything would be OK, and stared at the table when Dad began to weep.

"I should go," my mother said. "I would ask you to come with me, Lottie, but space is an issue and this is only for the very short term. Your father and I have a lot of sorting out to do, but we've agreed that you come first. Once we sell this house, we'll have enough money to provide you with two places you can call home."

"But I don't want to move," I said. "And I don't want you to go."

My mother rose from the table. She circled behind my father, touched his shoulder for a moment and then headed for the door. When she opened it, the howling I could hear out there sounded like another world entirely.

The first few nights were the worst. I suppose we had to get used to the loss and what it meant for us all. The winds struck at sunset and only calmed as dawn broke. In the darkest hours gusts would rampage across town and country with such violence that I couldn't sleep. The experts explained how this was due to the absence of a gravitational pull. As I looked at the impact around me, it seemed more like the loss of a calming influence.

On the television Dad and I watched endless news footage of tidal surges and oceanic whirlpools. It looked to me like God had got fed up with us all and decided to pull the plug. All my favourite programmes were replaced by reports about emerging changes to our planet. Birds flocked in unusual directions, clouds formed strange new shapes, and dogs howled after midnight as if plagued by a frequency beyond our hearing.

Even people behaved differently. Many panicked, with riots taking place as far afield as Reykjavik, Moscow and Rio de Janeiro. I also heard from Maisie that her neighbour had switched to a day shift on account of all the late night loot-ing. As for me, I found my hay fever disappeared completely.

At home our cat reacted badly to the situation. It didn't help that Mum was the one who had always taken care of him. After she left he went hungry for several days because Dad and I completely forgot to feed him. Worse still, the high winds really spooked the poor thing. Instead of spending his nights out on the prowl, he chose to stay indoors. Even with the calm that came at daybreak, he would pop out only for a very short time. Then he'd crash back through the cat flap as if chased in by a snarling dog.

"What's frightening him?" I asked on one occasion.

My father considered this for a moment, watching the fur on the cat's back settle. "Change," he said finally. "It's an unsettling time for us all."

Throughout this period, while most governments appealed for calm, the two superpowers continued to raise the temper-ature. In an address to the world President Reagan not only denied all involvement in the moon strike, but even went so far as to suggest that the Russians had been attempting a sur-prise attack on American defence satellites. One which had ended in a cosmic disaster for us all. As each side had primed their nuclear arsenal to take flight, I asked if we should pre-pare a fallout shelter. In response, Dad turned to me as if emerging from a dream, and said it was too late for that.

* * *

I was at school when Mum first returned to pick up some things. I knew she had been here as soon as I walked in. Her perfume hung in the air and the cat was at his bowl, finishing a treat of canned tuna.

Then, late last night, she came back again. I was in bed when I heard the key in the lock. Normally at that hour I'd have been asleep but, what with the high winds, I was wide awake.

I heard her close the door against the gale, and then her voice calling softly for my father. I wanted to get up and see her. I really did. I was just worried that by padding downstairs, somehow I would scare her away. A moment later, my parents were speaking in the kitchen.

It struck me then that Dad hadn't shown any anger about the situation. He wasn't like the president, whose emotions were quite clear each time he made a broadcast. Reagan didn't shout or beat the desk with his fist, but you could see it in his face. From a tension in his jawline to the way his eyes pinched when he outlined the American position. My dad didn't carry that kind of fire within him. Once he had stopped weeping, there was nothing left.

As I listened to them from my bed, it sounded as if my mother was doing all the talking. At one point I even heard some words.

"I'm sorry," she said. *"I'm just sorry."*

* * *

The storm that night was more ferocious than anything we had experienced. It raged so hard against my window that I was too scared to climb out and peek through the curtains. I just pulled my duvet over my head, and prayed the house would not be blown to bits.

Now, as sunrise sees the winds subside, I look out and catch my breath. Trees have come down everywhere, bringing power lines with them, while somewhere in the distance I can hear a voice droning through a megaphone. Weirdly, though, the street is deserted. I switch on my radio, if only for some company, and that's when I hear about the emergency measures.

"Dad!"

Grabbing my dressing-gown, I rush across the landing to the main bedroom. If the government really have ordered troops onto the street, there'll be no school today for sure. I don't pause to knock. I throw open the door and then stop in my tracks.

I'm surprised to find the cat curled up at the foot of the bed. My father is sound asleep, but what leaves me reeling is the sight of the woman in his arms. Her head is resting upon his shoulder, with her palm flat on his chest. She opens her eyes and looks at me. At first, we just gaze at one another.

"We've been ordered to stay inside," I say eventually, blinking back tears. "It's chaos out there."

Just then, from somewhere over the hills, we hear the crack of gunfire. The sound takes a moment to decay, as if refusing to fall silent.

"Things will never be the same again," says Mum in barely a whisper. "All we can do is hope that we're over the worst."

ONE GIANT LEAP

Philip Ardagh

In July 1969, Neil Armstrong became the first man to walk on the Moon…

There are countless monuments to the memory of US astronauts Neil Armstrong and Buzz Aldrin, with hundreds in the United States alone. The best known must be the Apollo 11 Memorial in Washington DC, and the Armstrong–Aldrin statue at the Kennedy Space Center. There are, of course, no graves in Arlington National Cemetery, where one would have expected such all-American heroes to be laid to rest. There were no grand funerals. No coffins draped with star-spangled banners or soldiers with heads bowed.

The silver-haired man had visited many of these monuments over the years, but it was to the one in Wapakoneta, Ohio, that he always returned. It is an enormous statue of an astronaut, at least double life-size but looking even larger up on its high plinth. It's of Wapakoneta's most famous son, Neil Armstrong: one of only two people ever to have walked on the surface of the Moon. The lifeless Armstrong stands proudly in his spacesuit, his goldfish-bowl-like helmet tucked under his arm, looking up with sightless stone eyes to the stars, where he sought adventure and remains for ever. This is the people of Wapakoneta claiming their own.

In July 2009, on the fortieth anniversary of the Moon landing, the man took yet another pilgrimage to Wapakoneta, quietly and anonymously, away from the bigger crowds of officials and dignitaries gathered in Washington and Houston, Texas. He stood in front of the Armstrong statue. Armstrong had not grown old as he had. The commander stays thirty-eight years old for eternity. He, on the other hand, was now seventy-eight. His military bearing was still evident, but his back no longer as rod straight as he'd have liked. Age has a nasty way of sneaking up on one like that. He looked at his shoes and saw that the leather was scuffed at the toes. He wished he'd thought to bring a newer pair – not that anyone would give him or his shoes a second glance.

It was early evening when he arrived, and the dying sun created a beautiful light in the wide Ohio sky, casting long, low shadows. He felt the faintest of breezes ruffle his hair, its usual silver made orangey-gold by the sun's final fading rays. The cuffs of his light blue shirt were worn, though not actually frayed.

A child laughed and began to circle the outer perimeter of the roped-off area around the statue's base, chased by a girl the man took to be his elder sister. The boy was clutching a toy space rocket while she had cotton candy on a stick.

She happily chewed on the pink spun floss as she roared after him.

The inscription at the base of the Apollo 11 Memorial in Washington DC reads: *Their deeds and their sacrifice were for all mankind.* The inscription on the Armstrong–Aldrin statue at Cape Kennedy states: *These brave men died not for their country but for humanity.* Both are quotes from President Nixon's address to the world, viewed by billions back in 1969.

Here in Wapakoneta, however, the words carved into the stone simply read:

NEIL ARMSTRONG

BORN: WAPAKONETA, USA, EARTH

AUGUST 5, 1930

DIED: THE MOON

JULY 21/22, 1969

There is no specific date given for his death because no one is exactly sure when the last of the oxygen ran out. The calculations have been made and debated a thousand times, but no one can say with absolute certainty which side of midnight he and Buzz died, so it is not writ in stone.

At their own request Armstrong and Aldrin ended all contact with Mission Control for their final minutes or hours. With the eyes and ears of all the world upon them, they were granted the one thing that their controllers back here on Earth could afford them: the dignity of a private passing.

Standing before the Wapakoneta statue, the silver-haired man reflected on how technology had changed beyond recognition in the intervening forty years. He remembered how the row after row of screens at NASA's Mission Control in Houston had seemed the very pinnacle of what computers could achieve. The safest pair of hands one could hope to be in. Now his washing machine contained more technological know-how than all of Mission Control's computers back then put together.

People from all over the world have visited Wapakoneta over the years and left flowers, cards and messages at the foot of the plinth. Many have run their fingers across Armstrong's name. These literally touching tributes have smoothed the once crisply carved letters' edges: a form of human-made erosion. They will be worn away long before his and Aldrin's footprints on the windless Moon. The two astronauts have become the icons and inspiration to adventurers and explorers in all walks of life. On that day in July 2009, there were more small personal tributes carpeting the ground than ever, along with official tributes from organizations, "personalities" and nations. The silver-haired man found himself leaning over the red rope and scanning the cards for familiar names.

Now he turned and walked back towards his car. Seeing him coming, the overweight driver had struggled out of his seat and opened his door for him. The man climbed in. There would be services throughout the US that weekend to remember the only two human beings ever to have walked on ground not belonging to their native planet, their having paid the ultimate price for that privilege.

The events of 1969 were for ever etched into the silver-haired man's memory. When he closed his eyes in the back of that car – as the last vestiges of warmth disappeared with the sun – the images were still acid-burnt into his retina, barely faded with time. He could remember everything so clearly. There was a cavernous void in the pit of his stomach.

He was not one of those who had huddled around a tiny television set at home or at a friend's or relative's, as was the experience of so many back then. He had sat alone, waiting like no other.

It is 20 July 1969 and the world watches, waits and listens as the lunar module *Eagle* separates from the command module *Columbia* and – after what seems a nail-biting eternity – lands on the Moon.

Time passes. Now, bouncing down the ladder of *Eagle* and onto the Moon's dusty surface, Neil Armstrong speaks the immortal lines: "One small step for [a] man, one giant leap for mankind" and changes history in a way that it has never been changed before.

Satellites may have been sent into orbit. Men and women may have flown into space and even have walked in it, but this was the first time a human being had left a footprint *on the Moon*. The unreachable had been reached. Suddenly a million other possibilities come into flower.

Suddenly the name of Yuri Gagarin, the first human in space, becomes secondary to that of Neil Armstrong, the first human on the Moon. Until now the space race has not been a proper race at all, with Russia easily winning at every level: first satellite, first person (a man), first woman, first space walk ... with the US's National Aeronautics and Space Administration lagging far behind. Now Russia's bubble has been burst. All other firsts will be all but forgotten. The rules have changed. Now the US can claim the ultimate prize...

...a prize about to be tarnished by tragedy.

After a total of twenty-one hours on the surface, it's time for Armstrong and Aldrin to leave the Moon and to rejoin Michael Collins, who is orbiting it in the command module. It is 1.54 p.m. Eastern Daylight Time on 21 July 1969 ... but nothing happens.

There is no graceful departure. No arched trajectory through space. Instead, a damp squib and a sinking heart. In Armstrong's own words, the engines of the module fail to "light up". Despite repeated efforts on the Moon and suggestions from Houston, the ghastly possibility that the astronauts may be doomed begins to sink in.

Then it becomes a reality. The module and the men inside are going nowhere.

Time slows to a standstill.

The empty hours are filled with mind-numbing speculation. The television is filled with talking heads not really knowing what to say. The world waits.

Then comes the announcement. The president of the United States of America is about to make an address. People tune in across the globe.

Waiting.

They are finally met by an image of a sweating President Nixon seated at his desk in the Oval Office. His voice breaking with emotion, he begins to speak the words he hoped and prayed he'd never have to utter.

"Fate," he says, "has ordained that the men who went to the Moon to explore in peace will stay on the Moon to *rest* in peace."

This single sentence – these twenty-four words – sends shock waves around the world. All sense of triumph and euphoria is snuffed out in an instant. The sickening possibility – unspoken by most – has become a dreadful reality.

To some the shock is so great that the next few sentences of the president are lost. He refers to Armstrong and Aldrin as "these brave men" and talks of sacrifice. Then, with shoulders back and real tears in his eyes, Nixon stares straight into the camera and says, "In ancient days, men looked at stars and saw their heroes in the constellations. In modern times, we do much the same, but our heroes are epic men of flesh and blood."

One of the billions watching the broadcast is William Safire. He sits alone in a borrowed office, shirtsleeves rolled up to the elbow, the only light coming from the flickering cathode ray tube. In his hands he holds a memo headed *In Event of Moon Disaster*. Silently he mouths the words as Nixon speaks them.

"Others will follow, and surely find their way home. Man's search will not be denied. But these men were the first, and they will remain foremost in our hearts."

These are Safire's words, crafted by his hands and put in the president's mouth. This is one presidential speech everyone in the White House had hoped would never have to be delivered.

The broadcast is nearly at an end. Nixon is reading the final words on the autocue: "For every human being who looks up at the Moon in the nights to come—" Then he breaks off. He struggles for something personal to say, not something pre-planned for a worst-case scenario, but something immediate and from the heart. He looks down at the copy of the speech on the Oval Office desk: typed and double-spaced. He lifts it up, shuffling the pages. Then he utters possibly the most famous words of his presidency.

"My fellow Americans," he says. "These brave men died not for their country but for humanity. Their deeds and their sacrifice were for all mankind."

After the address, there are the phone calls, conducted

off the international stage, away from the eyes of the world's media. Nixon has already made calls to the widows of Armstrong and Aldrin. He did that before the broadcast. As commander-in-chief, the president has had to make such calls before – to widows of other fallen servicemen – but never to the wives of such a unique brand of hero. Just twenty-four hours previously, Armstrong was the most talked-about man on the planet. Now Aldrin's name can be added alongside his. Had things turned out differently, he might just have been remembered as the second man to walk on the Moon, simply following in another's footsteps. As it is, their names will be linked for ever, as their bodies lie together in another place.

Then comes the final leg of this tragic journey: the return of Michael Collins, the third, forgotten, astronaut. Collins is the pilot whose job it was to orbit the Moon in the command module *Columbia*, while the other two set down upon its surface. With Armstrong and Aldrin dead, the top priority – the *only* priority – is to get him safely home.

His successful re-entry into the Earth's atmosphere and his retrieval from the space capsule in the sea are, in the end, a subdued affair. No one can paint him a hero, however hard they try.

There is nothing Collins could have done. There was no backup plan for if the lunar module engines failed to fire and it could not take off again – other than to have him return home alone. Despite this, many cannot forgive him for "abandoning" them, least of all Michael Collins himself.

He remains for twenty-one days in quarantine in a chamber intended for three. No witty banter for the camera or the company of colleagues. No conversation with his president via telephone as the two men watch each other through the glass. Heroes die with epic gestures. To many, Collins is seen as an embarrassing reminder of a nation's failure. He soon becomes a solitary figure, refusing to give interviews and leading the most private of private lives, blighted with survivor guilt.

Sitting back in the car now being driven at speed – putting as many miles between himself and Wapakoneta – he thought, for the millionth time, how different it would have been if they'd all come home together. He thought of an alternative history where *Eagle*'s engines had fired and docked with the command module and they'd all made it home. Instead of *this*.

As the Ohio countryside rushed past him, he looked up to the sky. Seeing the Moon, he pressed his hand against the window and spoke his nightly ritual.

"Goodnight, Neil. Goodnight, Buzz," he said, closing his eyes and wishing that, for once, he would have a dreamless sleep.

AUTHOR'S NOTE: Thankfully, in reality all three Apollo 11 astronauts returned home safely and are still alive at the time of writing. Although President Nixon never needed to make such a speech, that is not to say that the speech itself is fiction. It really was written by William Safire, to be used in the event of such a catastrophe. A full transcript is in the public domain and can be found in the US National Archives. I must also stress that, although I used the names of real people in this story, I am in no way suggesting that the actual people would have behaved in the manner in which I describe.

THE Y2K BUG

Eleanor Updale

As the twentieth century came to an end, a warning of doom ran round the world. People said that computers would not be able to cope when their internal clocks changed from 1999 to 2000. There were dire predictions that crucial services and communication links might crash.

In 1999 there were no iPods, and many households still had neither a computer nor a mobile phone, but "new technology", as it was called then, had made an impact everywhere in a rapid, uncontrolled way. The industrial, political and business worlds already depended on microchips, so governments across the world treated the threat of the "Y2K Bug" seriously, and took precautions.

In the event, they probably felt rather foolish as midnight on 31 December 1999 came and went without incident.

But what if it hadn't?

(Sorry, I've lost track of the date)

It's going to take me ages to type this. I'm using Gran's old manual typewriter. I'm not used to having to hit keys so hard, and it took me a long time to work out how to load up the ribbon. I've got ink all over my hands. But I want to type it. I don't want the people of the future to have to decipher my handwriting. And, anyway, we've only got a few pencils left now, and pencil writing smudges and fades. I want this to last. I want to set down what has happened – at least as much as we can work out here. Because one day someone might find this and it might explain the things they can't understand...

It sounds mad, but we knew it was going to happen. The papers had been going on about the Y2K Bug for months.

They'd shown all the precautions the government had in place, and the public had been getting ready for computer trouble. I'd even printed out my coursework just in case. (It was a project about international trade routes. It was geography then – it's history now.) I'm typing this on the back of it. We can't afford to waste paper these days.

And it wasn't just in the press. We actually *saw* it making its way towards us on the telly. There were special programmes all day on New Year's Eve, showing midnight sweeping from east to west across the world, starting somewhere way down under. Tonga, or somewhere like that. I'd check; except I can't. Not now. It's not as if I can go on the Internet, or even down to the library. Anyway, by lunchtime the TV news was running pictures of one place after another having a party and then going dark: New Zealand, Australia and countless other countries I'd never heard of. The reports were followed by interviews with British government ministers, who kept telling us not to panic: they had plans in place for midnight GMT.

In our house we had good reason to believe them. My dad worked in IT at the power station. He already knew that he would have to go to work that night. He was annoyed about missing the celebrations. But he was confident that the plant would cope, even if the doom-mongers turned out to be right and its many computers did go down for a while. So Mum hadn't joined the bands of people who'd decided to do some last-minute stocking up on tinned food and bottled water. The message on the telly was clear: some faraway places were having a bit of a Y2K hiccup, but everyone was sure that they'd have themselves up and running again soon. Meanwhile, it was over to Davina McCall and the jolly crowds outside the Millennium Dome who were gathering early in the hope of seeing the Queen and getting a good spot to watch the fireworks at midnight.

Through the afternoon there were a few reports on TV of people rushing to airports and harbours in search of transport westwards, to places where the new century would arrive a little later. A guest in the studio noticed a prominent politician and a minor royal in one of the check-in queues. The programme swiftly cut back to Davina and didn't return to the airport story.

I suppose we should have realized then that there really was something to worry about. But by that time, Mum had got us all helping to make the sandwiches for our street party, and Dad was leaving for work. If I'd known it was to be the last time I'd see him, I'd have said a proper goodbye. But my friend Fergus had come round to have a go on Donkey Kong on the Nintendo 64 I'd got for Christmas, and I didn't want to look wet. So when Dad said, "Have some candles ready for when it all goes black at midnight" we all just laughed.

So you see, we were warned. But no one wanted to take it seriously.

* * *

At midnight we were all outside in the street, high on the hill looking out over town. It was a balmy night. Not really cold at all. I found myself talking to neighbours I'd hardly met before. Everyone was happy and friendly, even the lady from number ten, Dr Parker, who had once told me off for dropping a crisp packet in the street. Mr Miller had run an extension lead out through his front-room window and set up a little telly on his garden wall, so we could see Big Ben doing its chimes. In the build-up to midnight, the security at the Dome went wrong and the glitterati of London all got stuck in Tube stations waiting to be let out. It was quite funny really.

"Looks like the Millennium Bug has struck early." Mum laughed. "I'm all for it, if it gives that lot a taste of what it's like to use public transport these days!" But she knew it was just good old-fashioned British incompetence. The kind we dream of now.

At about 11.45 p.m., the telly people interrupted their coverage of the big party to run a statement from the Prime Minister. He looked ahead to the new century and its promise of prosperity and peace. He slipped in some reassurance about any technical glitches that might happen at midnight. They would only be temporary. There was no need to panic. Mrs Miller was staring at the screen. "He's said that once too often," she mumbled, sounding worried. But no one took any notice and we all filled our glasses for a toast.

The cameras cut to Big Ben. The long musical chimes started, escorting out the final seconds of the year. Then there was the pause before the first big bong. But where that bong should have been there was only silence. Silence and darkness. A darkness like we'd never known. The TV screen was black. The streetlamps had gone out. Down in town there were some car headlights on the move, but very few, and they quickly flashed away. Most people were asleep, or celebrating. Looking up, I could see more stars than ever before.

And then the fireworks started. With all the lights out, it was the best display I'd ever seen. Fountains of colour burst out against the black sky. We drank and shouted, and when the explosions were over and we still couldn't get the telly going, we drank some more and rammed candles into the empty bottles to light our way indoors. Everyone gathered by an open fire in the Millers' house, surrounded by torches and candles. Mrs Miller played the piano, and we laughed together for hours, joking about the power cut, until gradually we each found our way home to sleep. Fergus led us down the street by the light of his new mobile phone. "It's all it's good for," he said. "I can't get a signal."

When I woke up, late the next day, I had forgotten about the blackout. I tried to turn on my computer, but it was dead. I went to call Fergus to see if his house had any power, but the phone line was out too, and the radiators were cold. I went into the kitchen. The kettle wouldn't switch on. The fridge was silent and dark inside. I swigged the last of the milk. It still had a slight chill to it. Then I went up to see if Mum and Dad were awake. But Dad hadn't come home from work. Things must be worse than he'd expected. We tried the transistor radio. Nothing.

"Maybe the one in my car will work," said Mum. "The battery gets charged by the engine."

So we went outside – me in my slippers, her still in her dressing-gown – and sat in the car, trying to tune in. But there was only crackle and hiss.

"The BBC must be putting out something," said Mum. "They have emergency generators for times like this. Lots of buildings do. Hospitals. Places like that."

I looked across the town. Sure enough, there were lights on in the hospital. They were on emergency power.

"Let's go down there. They'll know what's going on," said Mum, starting the engine with no thought to what she looked like. "We can get some more petrol on the way, so we can keep the car battery going."

But other people had had the same idea. There was a tangle of traffic round the petrol station, and a frightened man was sticking up signs saying NO POWER. PUMPS OUT. NO PETROL. Mum wriggled the car round and set off towards the hospital. It was the same there. The car park was full, and a traffic jam was snaking round the block. It was as if the whole town had been lured towards the hospital lights. We parked a few streets away and walked towards the casualty department. A man was standing on a box, shouting to the crowd outside. I recognized him. He was a local councillor, Mr Lambert. He'd given out the prizes at my school. He was a pompous prat. His hour had come.

"Order. Order please, ladies and gentlemen!" he was saying. "Everything is under control. Emergencies only now, please. The hospital is under great strain. They've got power, but no phones and no computers. They can't call up anyone's notes. They can't run the new X-ray machines and scanners. And you can't come in just to keep warm. Go home now and put on some woolly clothes. Everything will be back to normal before you know it." He looked at my mother in her dressing-gown. "Are you a patient here, madam?"

"Good Lord, no!" squealed Mum, suddenly aware of her nightclothes. We ran back to the car and zoomed home. We saw a gang of men walking towards a darkened television shop. They were carrying iron bars and looked ready to smash their way in to grab what they could.

"Someone should call the police," said Mum. But then she remembered that the phones were out and nobody could.

"We could go to the police station," I said.

"If they hadn't closed it down," said Mum. "They thought it wasn't worth having so many so close together when everyone could keep in touch by phone and in cars. They weren't thinking about times like this. I'm not wasting petrol driving miles just to fetch the police. We're going to have to save fuel. This might go on for days."

And it did. For far more than just days. And it stopped being fun or interesting and started to get boring and frightening at the same time. For a little while the neighbours who had enjoyed New Year's Eve together supported each other in their torment. Food and firesides were shared. But on the second weekend we woke to a familiar bottom disappearing over the back wall. We got downstairs and found the last of the Christmas Stilton gone.

Gradually everything that needed recharging ran out of power – you couldn't even use a mobile phone as a torch. Those men who had raided the TV shop had chosen the wrong target. People were stealing batteries and gas bottles and boxes of matches now. The water stopped running, and sewage started backing up out of the drains. We cleaned ourselves with baby wipes, until they ran out and we just stayed dirty. People took plastic bottles to the swimming pool and collected the stale chlorine-laden water to drink.

At first, police cars toured the streets, looking for looters. They kept hungry families out of Tesco while food rotted in the dead freezers. Then the police ran out of petrol too, and requisitioned bikes – riding around, armed, to shoot thieves. Within weeks, the uniformed men on bikes became looters themselves, to feed their families. Anything they couldn't eat they sold at extortionate prices. I asked my mum why they were doing it, when they were supposed to be in charge.

"It's hard for anyone to be good at a time like this," she said, "especially when you have a family. And it must be difficult to be a good policeman when you are a family man with a gun."

People walked to nearby towns to get help and came back with rumours. It wasn't just our town. Things were bad everywhere. There was news of the underground bunker near Bath, built long ago to house important people after a nuclear attack. Before the Bug it had been a top-secret place, known only to the Great and the Good: those with jobs of national importance. The trouble was, when things got tough, the Great and the Good had brought their families with them for shelter, and their numbers were added to by everyone who had been Great and Good in the past. Former officials, former ministers and two former prime ministers had all remembered the secret address to which they had once been privy. Soldiers had to guard the door. Shots had been fired. Famous people were dead. And the bunker was no use anyway, because there was no way of getting food in or messages out.

I asked about the power station. I wanted to know if anyone had seen my dad. Someone said there'd been an explosion. I didn't know what to believe.

* * *

And of course we should have gone back to school. It was due to reopen on Tuesday 11 January. I actually went. I even wore my uniform. For once I didn't mind: those were my cleanest clothes. They'd been washed before Christmas. But school didn't open. That councillor was there, turning pupils away. He said it was a "health and safety" matter. It wasn't safe for us to be together in large numbers without heat, light and water – and in any case, most of the teachers hadn't turned up.

The only place people could gather was in church. The second of January had been a Sunday, and vicars all across town had seized the opportunity for an illustrated sermon about the wages of sin. Soon the ringing of a church bell became the signal for people to come and hear the latest news from a traveller who had staggered in from another town, or to share some newly discovered food. But within weeks some of the vicars had been ousted by parishioners with more lurid interpretations of what was going on. And there were splits between the churches. One started worshipping the International Space Station, which was still orbiting, reflecting the sun and standing out as one of the brightest objects in the night sky. Its members interpreted obscure passages in the Bible to show that the astronauts onboard were not marooned, or dead, but waiting to return and redeem mankind. Another congregation started planning a trek across

land and sea to Africa. They argued that low-tech societies
would have survived the computer crash and would eventually come to save us, if only someone could tell them the
mess we were in.

My neighbour, Dr Parker – the one who had told me off
about the crisp packet – was behind that plan.

"You see, where we went wrong as a society," she said,
in the confident voice that had once served her well as a
university lecturer, "was to let the technology take over. We
got to the point where computers weren't just a help – they
had become essential for even the most mundane of tasks:
the exchange of money; the distribution of food, fuel and
the mail; the production of newspapers; the transmission of
radio and television signals. Take away the technology and
what were once simple operations become impossible. We
will have to learn to live like primitive men again."

"You mean like people in the 1950s?" said Mum. "We
didn't have any computers then."

Dr Parker was thoughtful. "Well, we may need to go back
a lot earlier than that. To relearn skills we have all lost."

Half an hour later, there we were: Dr Parker, my mother and
me, breaking into the museum by the back door. We stared
at everything from warming pans to butter churns, and wondered what to take. In the end, the three of us lugged an old
plough back home, ready to cultivate our gardens if things

weren't back to normal by the spring. Meanwhile, others were ransacking the library next door. They weren't choosing books for their rarity or interest – simply for how well they would burn. Dr Parker drew the line at that.

When we got home, I found myself searching for one particular book. I had bought it for Dad as a joke present that Christmas. I'd never really thought it would come in handy, but what better title could there be now than *The SAS Survival Handbook: How to Survive in the Wild, in any Climate, on Land or Sea*. I silently thanked the author, John "Lofty" Wiseman, and wondered how he was getting on, wherever he was. Perhaps he and the SAS would manage to sort everything out, somehow.

"That's what I can't understand," said Dr Parker when I showed her the book. "Where is the army? Where are the politicians? Why hasn't anyone taken control? You'd think that in any human society someone would rise to the top."

"There's Councillor Lambert," said Mum. "You see him all over town, trying to run things."

"Trying to *stop* things, you mean," said Dr Parker. "He's always closing places down, sending people away. I bet he'd shut the hospital if an epidemic broke out."

And he did, of course. As vomiting and diarrhoea spread through the town, Councillor Lambert decided that the hospital would become an epicentre of infection. He refused to let sick people inside. It hardly mattered, though. There was no medicine left, fuel for the emergency generator had run out, and most of the staff had already decided to stay away from patients for the sake (or so they told themselves) of their families. As people lost the energy to dig even the shallowest of graves for the dead, the groups of people praying to the Space Station grew larger every night. They implored the astronauts to descend and save us.

That would have been surprising enough, but no one was prepared for the strangers who did eventually come.

I think I may have seen them first. It was very early in the morning. I was out guarding the potatoes in the yard when I saw what looked like a horse-drawn cart. It was a cart all right, but instead of horses, it was being pulled by twenty or so half-naked, weary men. Their masters in the carriage wore long robes, headdresses, and had flowing beards. Beards are not an unusual sight these days – even I have one, of sorts, and Dr Parker doesn't bother to pluck the straggly black hairs on her chin any more – but the beards on these men were luxurious, well-tended: an indication of status rather than desperation. These men were in command. You could guess that just from how they looked, from how clean they were, but the heavy rifle each of them carried left no room for doubt.

I was lucky. The tightly clipped hedge that had once marked the boundary to our front garden was now over-grown, and I was able to hide behind it and watch the strange vehicle go past. Up close, I could see the faces of the team hauling the carriage. They were oddly familiar. I knew I had seen them somewhere before. On television, perhaps? Was this the filming of some new extreme reality show? Were there hidden cameras? Had some cruel director been watching us in our distress? I tried desperately to place the faces. It was no good. I couldn't remember their names.

But a moment later, I could recall what they did. They were the Prime Minister, the Foreign Secretary, the Chancellor of the Exchequer and several other politicians familiar from a thousand boring bulletins. Here was the British Cabinet, the party people from the Millennium Dome, paraded in chains and shamed.

A tall man, who was holding the reins, pulled his slaves to a halt. He gave instructions to the other men in the carriage in a language I could not understand, and pointed towards the centre of town. Then with a slap from his whip he steered the cart in the direction of the school. There was no one around. The cart entered the playground, and a dozen fit, armed sentries took up position, their guns pointing through the railings at the surrounding streets.

I had to go. I had to take something to those poor enslaved men. They needed water. They needed food. I dug up some turnips and carefully poured rainwater from one of the museum chamber pots into an old plastic bottle left over from the millennium party nearly two years ago. I knew

I would probably get caught, but this might be my only chance to find out what was going on. Perhaps the slaves would know what had happened to my father. Maybe they could tell me how to get us all out of this mess.

I knew the back way into school from years of turning up late and sneaking through the cookhouse. I kept away from the window of the headmaster's study, where I could see the leader of the captors, pacing. At last, I heard a familiar voice coming from the gym. It belonged to the Deputy Prime Minister, and he was complaining that he was hungry.

Keeping as low as I could, so that the guards in the playground wouldn't spot me, I slithered up to the gym door, which was slightly ajar. I could see the slaves lying on the ground, resting. I managed to attract the Deputy Prime Minister's attention. If I hadn't heard his voice, I would never have recognized him. His huge bulk had melted away, leaving behind flaps of flabby skin around his face and stomach. He kept talking as he rolled towards me. The guard in the gym was obviously used to his moaning, and took no notice. When the starving man was within reach, I passed in the raw turnips. He sank his teeth in. He swigged some water from the bottle.

I couldn't waste time. "Quick," I said. "Tell me. Who are these people? Why have they brought you here?"

"They are some sort of terrorists," he said. "They've kept us on the go for more than a year and a half now. Ever since that night at the Dome. They had it all planned. They took a chance that the Millennium Bug would turn out to be real, and had people standing by everywhere, ready to destroy power stations, army bases and broadcasting centres as soon as everything started to fall apart. And we politicians were all in one place, of course, just handy for them to swoop on."

Suddenly I could believe the story of the explosion at the power station. I knew that my father would not be coming back.

The Minister was still talking: "Now they're going round the country checking that there's no prospect of getting things back together. In every town they round up the young, able-bodied people, and shoot them. You must hide. You must find a way of getting the message out about what's happening. There are pockets of resistance. We've heard about them. People like you have managed to reach us with news. Some truckers in Derby even managed to get an old CB radio transmitter going. It did no good. There was no one to pick up the messages." He took another bite out of the turnip. I was worried that the guard would notice. The Minister's chewing was louder than his whispering. "If only we'd known. I can't think what the intelligence services were doing. We didn't have any warning of this at all."

I knew I couldn't risk staying for long, but I had a few more questions. "What do these people want?"

"Well that's something I do know. They go on about it enough. They're not after anything we can bargain over.

They want to destroy our way of life. They despise us and everything we stand for."

"And how did they know their plan would work? Did they plant the Millennium Bug? Was it some sort of virus?"

"No, it was real, but accidental. A weakness built into the design of early computers. We had to warn people about it. The trouble was that by raising the alarm we gave Bin Laden his big idea."

"Bin Laden?"

"The boss man. The tall one. The one with the crazy eyes."

"But wasn't it a great risk, them planning all this? Weren't they afraid of getting caught? What if the Millennium Bug had let them down?"

"They had other plans if this one didn't work. Bin Laden would have stopped at nothing to knock us out. Apparently he even had some people training to fly planes into the World Trade Center in New York. He thought that would send us into an orgy of repression and surveillance, killing our own civilization from within."

"No need for that now," I whispered.

The guard snuffled. He had fallen asleep.

The Deputy Prime Minister had another nibble of the turnip, but he kept talking. "You get away and hide, son. Go while he's not looking. I'd come too, but I haven't the energy, and they'd only take it out on the others."

"Shoot them?"

"If only. That would be kinder. No, they'll make them dance together naked, or something like that. There's no limit to the humiliations they subject us to in the name of their cause."

I wanted to ask more questions, but he shooed me away. "Go on. Run. They'll probably find you, but give yourself a chance – and do anything you can to pass on the word about what's happened."

I crept away, up the hill. Mum has been low lately, spending most of the day in bed, and she was still asleep when I got back. I knew that Bin Laden's men would be with us soon, but there was no need to wake her just to tell her of new horrors ahead. What could she do about them? There's no point running away. Where would we run to?

So that's why I'm here in the attic with Gran's typewriter. I'm trying at least to leave some record behind. Not exactly Anne Frank, I admit. I've only been up here a few hours, and I'm sure my neighbours will shop me to the enemy as soon as the men arrive. But I'll put this paper in a plastic bag now, and then into a jar to keep it dry. A sort of message in a bottle, just in case any future generations are interested. Just in case anyone ever wants to know the true story of the Y2K Bug.

AT THE BALL GAME

Frank Cottrell Boyce

The Aztec civilization was decimated when the Spanish explorer Hernán Cortés invaded and colonized Mexico in the sixteenth century. One of the ancient beliefs of these doomed people was that the world will end in December 2012…

onkey8 was the last in line. She was the only girl, the smallest and the most excited in her Ten. The others had all played the game on real courts before; she had only played on the school court and in the alleyways and covered walkways of her home. They were trotting in now, under the shadow of the great arch of the New Court. She paused, took a breath, tried to steady herself. Then she too ran into the arena. The sound: the cheers of the crowd that broke over her like a wave; the colours: the wet red of the playing surface, the gold around the spectators' necks; the shadows: the black circle in the heart of the scoring hoop, the deep, concealing shade of the stands – everything was louder, sharper, brighter, than anything she had seen before. It was so beautiful she felt she could barely move. She wanted to stand and look at it for ever.

Then she saw the ball. It was already in play, spinning towards the ring. And then she was moving too. The ball bounced off at a crazy angle and everything about her was connected to it. Her brain was calculating its trajectory; her eye was following its flight; her feet were moving into the space without her having to think about it. Even though her eyes were on the ball, she was also aware that Jaguar3 of her own team was going for it with his left elbow, and somehow she knew that he had spotted her and would pass it to her. She stopped and turned, ready to take the ball with her right hip and pass it forward. She braced herself for the hurt and said a prayer to her guardian, the Nocturnal Monkey.

All this took less time than it took for the hard rubber ball to fall ten feet. Jaguar3 jumped, offering his chest to the rocketing ball. But instead of twisting and sending it to her, he yelped and fell, as though shot. He lay on the ground, clutching his chest in agony while the ball bounced once, twice, three ... too many times. They had lost the ball. It belonged to the other Ten now.

Jaguar3's brother went to help him up while the other players – from both teams – just stood and laughed at him. The spectators laughed too. Monkey8 tried to join in but her eye was fixed on the great bruise that was already blooming on Jaguar3's chest. Mungo had told her that the ball they used on the New Court was harder than the school one and that the red surface was faster than the wooden floor. She had shouted at him and said he was only trying to scare her. Obviously he was right. She wondered if he was right about the other things too.

Then the ball was in play again and she was no longer thinking thoughts, only moves. They were going for the scoring hoop again; their scorer was beautifully placed. She thought about running over and scratching him but the ball was quicker than she was. He jumped for it, and the next thing she knew, it was curving perfectly through the centre of the scoring hoop. He threw up his arms in delight, but instead of cheers a loud booing filled the stadium. It sounded like some monster coming nearer. The scorer had kicked the ball with his foot. He probably hadn't meant to; sometimes it just happened. But he knew he'd done it now. He kneeled down and bowed his head and allowed his team captain to strike him on the back with his great wooden club. The crowd loved that.

Lord Tekokiztakitl himself threw the ball back into play – in the Final it would be the king. The ball went high into the air, where the gods could decide who should have it.

The gods decided on Monkey8. Now that it was coming to her, she was not afraid. She leaped high; she broadened her chest. The ball struck like a fist but she controlled it. She knew where Jaguar3 was. She knew the others were not watching him because he was dishonoured, so she flipped it to him. He flung his hip at the ball and it curved back into the air. She knew where it would go and was there waiting when it arrived. She caught it with her knee. She bounced it three times, killing its spin. They were coming at her; their captain had his club raised.

It was too late. She pulled back her leg and kneed the ball confidently through the middle of the stone scoring hoop. Then, for honour only, she trapped it on her chest as it dropped through the other side, softly as fruit.

The cheer she won then made the earlier cheers sound like mutters. Lord Tekokiztakitl stood up, so everyone else stood up. He took his gold ornaments from around his neck and she ran to receive them. Because he had done it, others did it, and she walked around the pitch allowing people to drape her with gold.

She was the first girl ever to score on a New Court. Surely they must let her play in the finals.

– It wasn't a dream, was it?

  – You mean you have dreamed of this before?

  – No.

  – Because that would mean something if you had.

  – No.

  – It might also mean something if you never had.

The Interpretation were questioning her. It was part of how they decided whether she would go through to the finals. Everyone said the Interpretation were scary but they seemed lovely. They bought her a cactus syrup at a street cafe in the shade of the New Court. She sat and watched the painters finishing the new mural. The New Court had been built specially for the 2012 finals. The mural showed scenes from the whole history of Aztec Europa. There was

Montezuma floating into the River Clyde on his imperial raft, over five hundred years ago, his huge nodding feather headdress making him look eight feet tall. No wonder the ghostfolk who lived here – with their pale speckly skin – thought he was a god. Apparently their god walked on water. Montezuma's raft was so low in the water, it looked like he was doing just that. They thought their god had come back to them.

– Where did you learn ulama? asked the man from the Interpretation.

– My father is a rubber importer. He gave me my first rubber ball to play with when I was five. The ghostfolk who work in our house and gardens have a boy, and he was for-ever kicking a fitba – those pig's bladder ghostfolk balls that hardly bounce. They kick it with their feet. When he saw how a real ball bounces, he couldn't leave it alone. We've played all day. Every day. Ever since. Father is busy; my mother is dead. We play in the corridors and in the delivery alley.

– You learned ulama from a ghostboy?

– We learned together. His name is Mungo.

– We don't need to know the ghostboy's name. You know that most of the players who are on the list for the finals are from great families? They were taught by other great players. One of them was taught by Neza himself. And Neza has declared him the greatest player he has ever seen.

– Let me play him and we'll see.

– This will be a game of universal significance. No girl has ever played in such a game. And a girl who learned her ulama skills in an alleyway ... you must admit it seems unlikely.

– Unlikely things are mostly from the gods, she said.
– Look at Montezuma. He went for a ride on the imperial raft one day, got caught up in the Gulf Stream and ended up here in a village called Glasgow. He founded the second empire and made that village into the greatest city on earth.

– You are comparing yourself to Montezuma?

– My father said we should all strive to be like him. So, yes, I compare myself to him. Every night before I sleep, I ask myself, did I do as Montezuma would have done?

– And how do you answer?

– When he was adrift, he was not scared. He didn't try to paddle back. He knew the gods were taking him somewhere, so he stood calm and strong like a god; and when he came here, they took him for a god. All I ever wanted to do was play the game. When I got older and I heard that no one born in the month of the Monkey had ever played in the New Court, I still played. When I realized that no girl was ever allowed to play, I still played. When my father tried to stop me, that was like the waves and the winds and the monsters that Montezuma fought. I still played. If the gods had made me want something so wrong, it must be because they had some purpose. I stood tall.

– So you lied to your father?

– Yes.

– You had better tell him the truth now. Because you will be playing in the semi-final and all the world will know.

She burst into tears when they told her, and they had to remind her that weeping was a beating offence.

She tried to remember all she had said to the Interpretation. After all, if she had convinced them, she should surely be able to convince her own father. When she got home, he had already heard. Before she could say a word, he had locked her in her room. She tried to sleep, hoping to dream of the Final. Then she sat up suddenly. Something was tapping at the window. She saw the pale freckly face pushed up against the glass.

– Mungo, she whispered and opened the window. – He won't let me play in the semi-final. It's so unfair.

– He's sacked my father and sent us away. He says it's all my fault, that I taught you ulama.

– At least your father will get another job and another house. I will never have another chance to play the game.

Mungo laughed at her. – A spoiled wee idiot, he called her.

– Do you know why it's called the Final? Because it's the final game. The gods are going to destroy this world and start a new one and everyone's going to die.

– No one's going to destroy the world.

– Yes, they are. The gods destroyed the world before,

once by flood, once by fire, once by the great wind, and once more by fire; and this year they will do it again. And that's why we're playing the Final, to thank them for letting us live so long; and maybe if the game is good enough, they will destroy us with something comfortable, like petals or snow, and not sores or locusts.

– Our God telt us that he'd destroy the world no more. Never again. He did it once and promised he'd never try that again. He put a rainbow in the sky to seal the deal.

– But your god is weak. He lost. Even before Real People came here, your god was nothing but a dead man nailed to a piece of wood. Your god is dead. Our gods will destroy the world and I will have missed my last chance to play.

– You played today.

– Mungo, it was so beautiful.

– You scored?

– But that wasn't it. It was the pitch, and the people, and the feeling of twenty of us watching the ball, and the ball seemed like a bird that knew its own mind and was testing us, asking us questions... I felt like I had come home. I wish you'd been there to see me.

– Come on. Climb out of there. Come and show me.

He put his hand out to help her through the window.

– Wait, she whispered. She collected all the gold that they had given her when she scored and stuffed it into her backpack.

He showed her handholds and footholds in the ancient

wall – the house had been one of the first to be built after the Aztecs landed. The king himself would come and look at it during the preparations for the Final.

– How d'you know where all these cracks and crannies are? she asked.

– I just do, he said.

And she knew from the way he said it that he had climbed up to her window and looked in before.

And so they ran away. They hid in the great drain that ran under the New Court. It was dry and dark in there, and they lay in the dark together and she thought of the playing surface spread above them like a blanket.

– How did you do?

– I scored. I don't mean points. I mean I put the ball through the actual hoop. Caught it when it landed too.

He smiled and went to sleep.

They crawled out of the drain at dawn and looked around the square. She was afraid her father would come.

– Come on, Mungo said. – Let's go. You've got gold. Let's run away.

– Why would I want to run away? It's the semi-finals.

– But you're rich. You don't need to play. Think of the places we could go. Tartary. Sheba. Anywhere. They say there is an undiscovered country way to the south. The people there can fly. It's called the Dreamplace.

– So? It's a dream. This is real. This is the navel of the

Cosmos. This is the New Court. And if I make it to the Final, the god Tekutizcatetal himself will be here, watching me. We won't see him; but he'll see me.

– If he's really a god, he can see you wherever you are. He can see you playing in Tartary or the Dreamland even. When it's just the two of us.

He was holding her hand too tightly. Did he really want to run away with her? Why didn't he want her to play in the finals? She yanked her arm free and cursed him.

– The gold, she said. – It's not me you want to run away with. It's the gold.

– What?

– It's just the gold you're after. Leave me alone. I will play and I will win. I'll be famous and I'll be rich.

She ran away from him, out into the square. At a cafe, in the shade, she saw the Interpretation and some others, drinking chocolate. When she got closer she saw that some of them were great players, famous players; she had a plastic model of one of them on her window seat at home.

She stood and watched them for a while. They seemed so confident and easy with each other. Then one of the Interpretation spotted her and called her over.

– Is it proper to sit here with you? she said.

– Of course, they replied. They were all smiles. One of them noticed Mungo and asked her if that was the ghostfolk boy she'd learned with.

– Yes, that's him.

She waved to Mungo to come and say hello – they were so nice; she was sure they would be fine with it – but Mungo was already walking away.

She stayed close to them after that. Even if her father came up to them now, he would not dare try to take her away from the Interpretation. She would play today.

And Neza would be playing today. The greatest player in two empires. She recognized him from his painting on the mural. It showed the spirit of Montezuma leading Neza by the hand onto the pitch at Rome. When Montezuma had arrived in Europe, the whole land had been full of wars. Before the Real People arrived the ghostfolk would fight each other over land, water, honour, religion, oil. Not just warrior on warrior either, but warrior on farmer, on women, on children. Tens of thousands, hundreds of thousands were murdered or starved or poisoned. Land by land, though, they learned ulama. They learned to settle their differences in the court, at the ball game instead.

At first they still wanted blood. That shelf next to the pitch where the scoring stones were lined up – in the early days that was where they put the skulls. The winning team used to slaughter the losing team and put their heads on that shelf. It made Monkey8 shudder to think of it.

But that was in the past, like war itself. For every nation now played the game. From Scotland to the great mountains over the sea and down into hot, brown India and over the greater mountains to the windy rice fields, everyone loved the game, and the beauty and courage of the players. And the bravest and most beautiful of all was Neza. When the tribes of Italy had threatened to rise up ten years ago, he had played for them against their enemies. Ten one-on-one games, one after the other. He had won every one. He had saved the world.

And today she would play against him.

This time she did not pause for breath before running onto the pitch. When she ran out the crowd roared her name, "Monkey! Monkey! Monkey!" They already had a song about her. She looked around and saw Neza standing there, just like in the mural, as though Montezuma was leading him on to the pitch. She wanted him to smile at her but he seemed not to see her. Maybe he was angry that the crowd were singing for her not him. She wanted to tell them to shut up.

But the ball was in play. So she wanted nothing now and all her thinking stopped. Her eyes were locked on the ball, her ears listening for her teammates. She knew none of them; she was the only one of her Ten who had qualified. This new Ten had arrived today from every quarter of the empire. When they called to her she didn't understand what they were saying. The only thing she understood was the ball.

The ball seemed to circle around Neza, as though he had some kind of gravitational effect on it. He brought his knee up and it whirled over his head towards her, but one of his Ten got a hip to it first and sent it curving up towards the stone ring. A girl. There was a girl on the other team too? A girl who was playing with Neza, feeding him passes, responding to his moves. Monkey8 hated her before she even saw her face.

The ball missed the ring but the girl was on it right away, throwing herself at it. Monkey8 jumped too. She pulled the ball down with her doubled-up knees, making her body into a kind of pouch. When she landed she had time to knee it up into the air, once for speed and a second time for direction. She sent it spinning across the court towards the scoring ring. Someone from her own team stopped it with his back and sent it back to her. She was nearer now, well in the zone. She stopped it with her shoulder and let it roll across her chest while she took her bearings. Then she saw the girl coming into her space.

Monkey8 shot. It was all she could do. She didn't even look until the ball was speeding away from her. It was heading straight for the ring. But suddenly Neza was there, in its path, as though the ball had spoken to him and told him where to be. All he had to do was jump. He could block it with his neck, with his shoulder. If he twisted a little he might even be able to make it hit the wall and score a point. She saw him jump; she saw that he was not looking at the ball. He was looking straight at her. How could he do that? How could he jump for the ball without even looking?

He couldn't. He missed. She scored.

There is no point trying to describe the noise in that stadium. She had defeated Neza. This time she did not walk around collecting gold ornaments; instead they threw them onto the pitch for her. She walked on golden litter. Her eyes turned to scan the crowd before she knew what she was looking for. Mungo. She wanted him to have seen. But also not to have seen. She knew that he could have done it just as well, but he would never be allowed to watch, let alone play. She looked for him anyway. Maybe it was because she did not want to turn and see Neza. Probably he hated her now. Probably he had walked off the pitch.

But when she turned round, there he was smiling at her. He rubbed her hair and pointed to her, and the cheering grew even louder. He bent down, whispered – Take care, little sister, and walked away. He didn't seem sad or troubled. He was waving to someone in the crowd. He seemed in a hurry to go.

– The Final is one-on-one. Do you realize that?

   – Me against Neza?

   – No, no. His luck has left him. Didn't you see? We are talking tonight. We will find someone more worthy.

As a player in the Final, Monkey8 was allowed to hang around the court as long as she wanted. She knew her father would not be allowed in, so she loitered in the concourse, accepting compliments and more gifts, all the while looking

out for Mungo. When she finally spotted him, she realized
he must have been there for a long time, watching her. She
shrugged.

He came over.

– Want to see the court? she said.

They went inside. There was no one else there. He
looked up at the scoring ring and she held up a rubber ball.

– This is the one I scored with.

– Give us a shot.

She threw it and he jumped, catching it on his knee and
sending it straight through the hoop first time.

Afterwards they lay down on the red playing surface.
The sky seemed to ripple into darkness. The moon rolled
over the lip of the court like a big red ball.

– We could play one-on-one. Just the two of us. It's my
court tonight.

– We've played one-on-one every day of our lives.

– Does my father know what I did here today?

– Aye. He's at home crying. He knows he can't get to you
now.

– Maybe he'll be proud when I win. Maybe he'll be
pleased when he sees the gold they gave me. Do you think
I'm richer than him now?

– Maybe.

– Let's play.

– Too tired.

– Too scared.

– Of you?

– I defeated Neza.

– He didn't want to win.

– Everyone wants to win.

– Not this game.

– *Especially* this game.

– Wait. You mean they haven't told you? You don't know what happens after the Final?

– Nothing. I told you: that's why it's called the Final. It's the final thing before the end of the world.

– The winner is the best player in the empire, right? Best person. So the winner—

– Will be me.

– The winner, they'll rip her heart out and offer it to the gods. To Tekutizcatetal or whatever, to see if they can change his mind.

– You're lying. Lying ghostdirt.

– Ghostdirt?

– How could you change a god's mind?

– By giving him your nice juicy heart to eat, apparently.

– It doesn't scare me. It's the Final. Everyone will die. If I die first, that's an honour. If Tekutizcatetal takes my heart, that is the greatest honour. Anyone would be proud.

– Not Neza, apparently, or else why did he throw the match?

– He did not throw the match; I defeated him. I scored. I won. I hate you.

– And I asked you to run away with me. And you didnae come.

She walked away but he followed. He grabbed her blouse and untucked it; then, taking the hem of his cloak, he knotted the blouse and the cloak together, just like the groom does to the bride when the Real People marry. They had played weddings sometimes when they were younger, but only when she wanted to. This was the first time he had started it. She laughed.

And then he said – We could still run away.

– No, we couldn't. I'm famous now.

– We could go in disguise. To the Dreamcountry. Say yes.

– Maybe I will.

They walked towards the great arch, where they found the Interpretation waiting for them.

– We are so glad to find you here, they said. – We have made our decision about tomorrow.

They were not threatening. They had no soldiers with them. But all the same, it was impossible to argue with them. It was as though the whole world, the way things worked, was talking through them.

– We thought about what you said, that the more unlikely something is, the more clearly it is a message from the gods.

– Did I say that?

– Yes. So we have decided that your opponent tomorrow will be this boy.

They pointed to Mungo.

* * *

They entered through opposite arches. He seemed unbelievably far away and unbelievably pale against the red surface. They had played one-on-one since they were five, so often that it was more like a dance than a game. They never kept track of who won. Today the winner would die and the loser would live. Today they were playing the same old game, but this time to the death.

She looked at him standing on the centre spot, and the sound of the crowd and the colours of the stadium seemed to vanish. Everything was as ghostly as his pale skin.

– We'll never see each other again after this.

– Good. You've bloody killed me. We should have run away.

– Let me win.

– Why would I do that?

– So I get killed and you don't. It's no great thing for me to die. I believe; you don't.

– I believe in doing the right thing. I'm going to win; you're going to live.

– Let me win. When the world ends, I'll be waiting for you at the door of the Good Place.

– *I'm* going to win. I'm not going to let them kill you. I'd rather be dead than see them kill you here.

– It doesn't make any sense. Let me win.

– You'll never beat me, because I won't let you. I'm playing for your life. Nothing will beat me.

* * *

The ball was in play. She missed it completely and realized she was watching him and not the ball, trying to remember him, a picture to take with her. The ball bounced high. Very high. She tried to wake up. She had to beat him. To save him. He was already running into position. The muscles in his legs coiled, ready to spring.

But then they both stopped. He was staring into the sky. She was staring into the sky. The crowd was staring into the sky. But not at the ball.

She was staring at the ... what was it? A thing like a cross, like the wooden thing that Mungo's weak god was nailed to. It was moving across the sky and making a noise, a coughing, choking noise. Like a weak thing. And it was coming nearer, falling out of the sky. In the stands people were screaming and scrambling out of their seats. But Mungo kept staring up. He made a sign like a cross on himself.

Then it was clear that the thing was going to land on the court itself. She dragged him out of the way as it struck the red surface. There was something on the front that whirled like an angry club, and smoke poured from the back. There was a thing like a single eye on the top; at least, she thought it was an eye, but then it opened and a figure stepped out. A male figure the same size as an Aztec man. Black like a man of Sheba, only blacker still. And his hair woolly and white. He stood on the wing of the thing and he waved! Just the way a man might wave. Everyone stood still and then waved back, imitating the god's wave. He waved again. They waved again.

This was it. The end of the world. Not a flood. But ... what? Waving?

The god began to speak, and everyone leaned forward to listen. The acoustics of the court were designed to amplify the dramatic thump of the rubber ball hitting the stone, so everyone heard everything he said but no one could understand a word. They shuffled a little, embarrassed that this was their god, come to talk to them, but they couldn't understand what he was saying.

Then slowly they began to enjoy the music of his talking and the fact that he seemed pleased to see them, and it dawned on them slowly that anyone who spoke with his relaxed, sing-song voice was very possibly not going to destroy the world after all. And as he waved again and they waved back again, they began to recognize certain words, because he said them a lot. Kuri, for instance, was his name. And Wollongong was where he was from. And aeroplane seemed to be the thing that took him into the air. He kept slapping it proudly.

While Kuri was talking, Mungo worked it out. This was not their god. This was not Tekutizcatetal, the destroyer of worlds. This was obviously *his* God. Obviously. He was even riding on a cross. Knowing that God was good, Mungo grabbed Monkey8 by the hand and dragged her over to the plane.

There was a gasp from the crowd. Was this it? Was the little ghost lad going to sacrifice her?

– All right, mate. Need a lift? said God.

Mungo did not understand the words, but he could see by looking into his eyes that this God really was good. And Kuri could see by looking into Mungo's eyes that Mungo was good. And the girl – she was digging her nails into the boy's hand and looking back at the crowd. They wanted to be together, that was clear too. The crowd. They were scared of the crowd. For some reason these kids had to get out of there.

– No worries, Kuri said. – Jump aboard. I'll sort you out.

He pushed back the glass bubble and pointed inside. They climbed in. It was cramped but Kuri pulled out some bags to make room for them.

– Don't worry. I'll dump this stuff. I'll miss it, but it's not the end of the world.

At first the crowd too somehow felt it wasn't the end of the world, as they watched their god – or some god, anyway – chugging up into the air on a tail of oily smoke, taking the two players with them. They waved and waved, but the more they waved the more they had the feeling that something really had ended; that they were saying goodbye not just to the players and the plane and the god, but to a world; that maybe they were saying goodbye to an old world and waving hello to a new one.

THE AUTHORS

Photo by Dotty Hendrix

Philip Ardagh

Roald Dahl Funny Prize winner Philip Ardagh has written over 100 books, both fiction and non-fiction, including *Grubtown Tales*, *Henry's House* and the Eddie Dickens adventures, which have been translated into over 30 languages. He collaborated with Sir Paul McCartney on the ex-Beatle's first children's book, *High in the Clouds*, and writes for radio and TV, as well as being a regular reviewer of children's books for the *Guardian*.

Frank Cottrell Boyce

Frank Cottrell Boyce won the 2004 Carnegie Medal for his first children's book, *Millions*. His screenplay of the same name was made into a film by Oscar-winning director Danny Boyle in the same year. He has since written three novels for children, including *Framed*, which was shortlisted for the 2005 Carnegie Medal and the Whitbread Children's Book of the Year Award.

Anthony McGowan

Anthony McGowan's novels for young adults include *Hellbent*, *Henry Tumour*, which won the 2006 Booktrust Teenage Prize and the 2007 Catalyst Award, and *The Knife That Killed Me*, which was shortlisted for the 2008 Booktrust Teenage Prize and longlisted for the 2008 Guardian Children's Fiction Prize. His latest book is *Einstein's Underpants – And How They Saved the World*. Anthony was born in Manchester, brought up in Leeds and lives in London.

Linda Newbery

Linda Newbery has published more than thirty titles, ranging from a picture book, *Posy*, to young adult novels, including *The Shell House* and *Sisterland*. She has twice been shortlisted for the Carnegie Medal, and won the 2006 Costa Children's Book Prize for her novel *Set in Stone*. *The Sandfather* was UK IBBY's nomination to the international Honour List for 2010.

Mal Peet

Mal Peet is the author of the critically acclaimed young adult novels *Tamar*, which won the 2005 Carnegie Medal, *Keeper*, winner of the 2003 Branford Boase Award, and *The Penalty*. His latest novel, *Exposure*, won the 2009 Guardian Children's Fiction Prize. He lives in Devon with his wife and fellow-writer Elspeth Graham.

Photo by Poppy Berry

Marcus Sedgwick

Marcus Sedgwick has written numerous award-winning books, including *Floodland*, winner of the 2000 Branford Boase Award, *My Swordhand is Singing*, which won the 2007 Booktrust Teenage Prize, and *Revolver*, which was nominated for the Guardian Children's Fiction Prize. His latest young adult novel, *White Crow*, was published in July 2010. He lives near Cambridge and has a teenage daughter, Alice.

Eleanor Updale

Having worked as a BBC TV and radio producer for many years, Eleanor Updale now writes fiction for all the family. Her *Montmorency* series has won international prizes, including the Blue Peter Award for "The Book I Couldn't Put Down". Her most recent book, *Johnny Swanson,* is a tale of murder and deception, set in 1929. She lives in London.

Matt Whyman

Bestselling author Matt Whyman is also well-known for his work as an advice columnist for numerous teenage magazines. His young adult novels include *Boy Kills Man*, which was shortlisted for the 2004 Booktrust Teenage Prize, as well as *Inside the Cage* and *Goldstrike*.